TALON

ALEXANDRA IVY

BAYOU HEAT

ALEXANDRA IVY

LAURA WRIGHT

Talon/Xavier
By Alexandra Ivy and Laura Wright
Copyright © 2013 by Alexandra Ivy and Laura Wright

Editor: Julia Ganis
Cover Art by Patricia Schmitt (Pickyme)
Interior Layout by www.formatting4U.com

PROLOGUE

LOUISIANA
1988

The house hidden in the tangled undergrowth just south of Bossier City was one stiff breeze away from total collapse.

Built from logs that had warped in the humid Louisiana weather, the cabin had a thin sheet of rusted tin and the windows were framed by rotting shutters. Even worse, the front porch had sagged at one end, giving it the appearance of a cheap funhouse.

Not the first place any man would select for his wife to give birth to his twin daughters.

But what choice did Chayton have?

With a muttered curse, he paced through the thick grass that left a damp film of dew on his knee-high moccasins. With the blood of the Chitimacha tribe flowing through his veins, Chayton felt most comfortable in soft leather pants and a vest that had been beaded by his mother. His glossy, dark hair was worn in a braid that fell to his waist, and his lean face was dominated by a prominent nose and eyes so dark they looked black. His bow was loosely held in one hand, with a quiver of arrows strapped to his back.

He was always on guard.

Ever since the vision had forced him to go on the run with his pregnant wife.

A familiar fear speared through his heart at the memory of that fateful day.

He'd been in the Wildlands at the request of the elders. He was one of the very few humans ever allowed in the remote sanctuary of the mystical Pantera. At first it had been his position as a shaman that had allowed him entry. Like his father before him, he'd had the ability to touch the spirit world.

It was a gift that gave him a much longer life span than most humans and the strange talent to detect the faction of an unborn Pantera baby. They called him when a female was close to delivering her cub to foresee whether it would be a Diplomat or Hunter or Healer. The Pantera began training their young from the cradle. Or at least they'd called him until the Pantera stopped having cubs.

That should have been the end of his connection to the Wildlands, but during one of his visits he'd stumbled across a talent that had only been a distant rumor among shamans until he'd manifested the gift.

He could do more than a catch a hint of the future of a Pantera.

He was an actual seer.

His predictions were often vague and sometimes impossible to interpret, but they were accurate enough that he was summoned to the Wildlands when the elders were debating a decision that would affect their people. Surrounded by the magic of the Wildlands, he would call upon the powers of his ancestors to be blessed with a glimpse of the future that could help lead the Pantera in the right direction.

It was a power he used only when the need was great.

Opening pathways to the ancestors was not only dangerous to him, but could occasionally allow malevolent spirits to escape into the world of men.

A damned shame he hadn't said no when the elders had called for him again six months ago. But then he'd never seen a vision that was so clear. And certainly never one so intimately connected to himself.

His dark thoughts were thankfully cut short as the midwife stepped onto the porch. A small, dried up prune of a woman, she was known by the locals as JuJu.

"It's done," she said in clipped tones, wiping her hands on a bloody apron wrapped around her thin body.

She had the bedside manner of a rattlesnake.

Chayton stepped forward. "My wife?"

"Weak, but she'll live."

"And the babes?"

"Both are healthy." The woman stuck out a hand gnarled by age. "You have my money?"

Chayton reached beneath his vest to pull out the precious money that he'd earned by selling the pelts of animals he hunted. He didn't dare take a job that would force him to fill out paperwork.

Paperwork could be traced.

He held up the money. "Your word that you won't speak of this birth," he growled, his eyes hard with warning. "Not to anyone."

A cunning expression touched her dark, leathered face. "It will cost you."

"Fine." Chayton added another fifty he couldn't afford. "Your word."

"You have it." JuJu snatched the money and poked it into the pocket of her apron. "Do you want to see your children?"

"Yes."

Chayton took a step forward only to come to a horrified halt when he heard a female voice speak from the nearby trees.

"We all wish to see the children."

In one fluid motion he had an arrow in his bow and pointed toward the strange mist that flowed forward.

"Stay back," he snarled, his gut twisting with dread as the mist lightened to reveal three females who moved forward with grim intent.

The elders.

He'd only seen them in their puma forms, but away from the Wildlands the females were forced to take human shape. Still, it was almost impossible to make out anything of their features as they deliberately used their powers to manipulate his mind. Once they left, no one would be able to describe more than slender, female figures and a choking power that made it difficult to breathe.

Fighting through his clouded thoughts, Chayton prepared to attack. The bitches would die before harming his babies.

Preparing to take his shot, Chayton was caught off guard as he was hit from behind. Knocked to the ground by two large men, he felt the bow knocked from his hand. Then, once his arms were painfully pinned behind his back, he was jerked upright.

A glance to the side revealed his worst fear.

Two dark-haired men with eyes that glowed gold in the fading light.

Pantera Hunters.

The elders waited until they were certain he was under the control of the Hunters before turning toward the stunned midwife.

"Take us to the children," they commanded in unison.

"Yes." Clearly under the influence of the elders, the midwife turned to walk back into the shack, her eyes unfocused.

The mist shimmered as the elders followed JuJu, making a gesture toward the silent Hunters.

"Bring him."

With a rough shove, Chayton was forced up the stairs and across the porch. A few more shoves and he was through the barren front room and into the back bedroom.

His breath was ripped from his lungs as he caught sight of his wife lying in the middle of the bed, a threadbare quilt covering her trembling body, and her pale hair damp with sweat. In her arms she clutched two tiny bundles wrapped in the blankets that Chayton had received from his mother as a birthing gift.

Her thin face turned in his direction. The past months hadn't been kind to Dixie. She'd thought marriage to him would mean a fine house and a position of honor in the small town of La Pierre. Instead she'd been forced to endure a difficult pregnancy living off the land like his ancestors.

Her eyes widened with confusion. "Chayton? What's going on?"

"Which child was born first?" the elders demanded.

The midwife reached to pluck one of the babes from Dixie's arms, pulling down the blanket to reveal the small birthmark on the child's collarbone.

"This one."

Shock rippled through the room as all eyes locked on the dark mark that marred the milky white skin. Even Chayton felt a twinge of unease.

"Ravens," the elders breathed.

The Mark of Shakpi.

No. It was just a birthmark. It was human nature to try and see a shape in what was nothing more than a blot.

Using his captors' distraction to his advantage, Chayton jerked free of their hold and lunged to take the baby from JuJu's arms.

"No," he rasped.

Dixie reached to grab the hem of his vest. "What are they doing?"

There was a low hiss from the elders. "The child is fated to destroy our homeland," they said.

"What?" Dixie's voice was shrill with fear. "She's just a baby."

Chayton clutched the baby to his heart. It was the first time he'd been allowed to cradle the sweet weight in his arms, but he'd loved his daughters from the moment he'd sensed that Dixie had conceived.

There was nothing he wouldn't sacrifice to protect them.

Including the future of the Pantera.

"We don't know that's what the vision meant," he rasped.

"What else can it mean?" the elders demanded, quoting back the words that had fallen from his own lips. "The blood of the Shaman's firstborn shall carry the taint of Shakpi, releasing her powers upon the lands of the Pantera."

He shook his head, stepping back. "You called me because your magic is already faltering. How can a newborn child be responsible for that?"

"Who is to say?" He had an impression of seething frustration just below the surface, although the elders continued to block his efforts to see beyond their magic. He was more immune than most humans to the mystic powers, so the fact they were able to keep him from seeing into their faces was annoying the hell out of him. Or maybe it was just a reaction to the fact they wanted to kill his daughter. "Perhaps we have failed in our duties," the elders continued. "Or perhaps time has weakened the bonds of Shakpi's prison."

"You would sacrifice the life of a babe on vague words that could mean anything?" He edged backward, sensing the door was only a few feet behind him. "Or nothing?"

"We must protect the Wildlands."

"A little late for your concern now, isn't it?" he charged.

There was a ripple of shock among the Pantera. "What do you mean?" they demanded.

Chayton lifted his chin. He'd had time to think over the past six months. He now realized that the elders had known all along how dangerous it was for him to open a direct doorway to the world of the dead. Which was no doubt why they left the task to the rare humans capable of manipulating the magic instead of trying to find a Pantera to perform the dangerous ceremony.

"You forced me to travel too often to the ancestors in your obsession to control the fate of your people, and allowed something evil to be released," he accused.

The air heated with the anger of the elders. "It's true we have discussed the possibility that Shakpi has used your journeys to the spirit world to infect you and now through you, your child."

Fury raced through Chayton. "Your arrogance created this disaster, and yet you would use an innocent baby to try and cover your asses."

There was a hiss of disbelief at his accusation before the elders moved toward him. "The sacrifice is demanded. Give us the child."

"Sacrifice?" Dixie clutched the younger twin in her arms, her face flushed. "Chayton, tell me what is happening."

The mist shimmered, as if annoyed by Dixie's interruption. "Sleep," they muttered.

Instantly Dixie fell into a deep slumber, the babe still tightly held in her arms.

Chayton bit back a curse at the sight of his wife's ready response to the command of the elders. Then, without warning, he was struck by a sudden, crazy plan.

His magic was limited, but he did have a small trick taught to him by his own father.

As the attention was turned toward the sleeping Dixie, Chayton reached into his pocket for the small flint he always carried. Then, concentrating his thoughts on the chiseled quartz, he felt it grow hot in his hands. Desperate, he poured every ounce of magic he possessed through his fingers and into the flint, waiting until the stone was searing his skin before he tossed it in the direction of the elders with a low word of ancient power.

On cue, the flint exploded into a searing white flame.

The elders cried out in shock while the two Hunters rushed to beat out the very real fire.

Instantly, Chayton was through the door and heading out of the house. He'd leaped off the porch and entered the nearby woods before the Hunters were on his trail.

Under normal circumstances a mere man wouldn't stand a chance against the lethal Pantera.

Even in their human forms they were stronger, faster, and their senses far more acute.

But Chayton wasn't just a man. He'd been trained by his father to become one with nature, allowing him to flow through the difficult terrain with a fluid ease. More importantly, he was far more familiar with the area than his trackers.

Choosing a route that would take him through marshy land so he could disguise his footprints as well as hide his scent, he ran as fast as his legs would carry him for a full hour. Only when he was certain the Hunters weren't about to tackle him from behind did he pause to carefully unwrap the blanket from the child in his arms.

Briefly he was distracted as the babe opened her eyes, regarding him with a solemn gaze that revived his flagging strength.

He was going to do everything in his power to protect his daughter.

With that thought, he pulled a dagger hidden inside the legging of his moccasin. Then, ignoring that trusting little gaze, he made a tiny cut on her foot. The babe let out a startled cry, but thankfully drifted back to sleep as he used the blanket to wipe the few drops of blood. He tossed the blanket into a nearby channel of water before making a much deeper cut into his forearm, swiftly smearing the blood on the mossy bank.

If he had any luck at all, the Hunters would believe he'd been attacked by an alligator or killed by some other predator.

If not…

He gathered the babe in his arms and took off.

If not, then he would keep running until the day he died.

CHAPTER ONE

THE WILDLANDS
2013

Moonlight glazed the lush foliage in silver as Talon crossed the boundary into the Wildlands. He stopped to take a deep breath, the magic in the air bubbling through him like the finest champagne.

Shit, he'd been gone too long.

Four weeks and two days to be exact.

He grimaced. He hadn't expected Parish's order to hunt for the traitors to lead him away from the Wildlands. It'd been enough of a shock to accept that there could be Pantera in their sanctuary who were willing to betray their own people. Hell, Parish had denied it even when the evidence was right in front of his face.

But after locking away Vincent and Savoy, and beginning his search for Pantera with the Mark of Shakpi branded on their heel, he'd learned that two Geeks had gone on the run, slipping away without leaving word with their families.

Talon had been in instant pursuit, at last tracking them to a cramped apartment in Baton Rouge.

A grim smile touched Talon's lean, starkly handsome face. He'd been pissed that he'd been forced to waste a month of his time tracking down the bastards, and even more infuriated that he might miss the upcoming Dyesse Fete—the celebration of the birth of the Pantera, and the most important holiday in the Wildlands.

Since the Elders had begun to notice the stagnant pools of decay at the fringes of their land it'd been feared that the tradition would die away. Just another sign that the Pantera were hovering on the brink of extinction. So it was hardly surprising that they each waited with baited breath each summer for the bloom of the purple water lily that would trumpet the beginning of the festival.

Still, when he'd entered the apartment he'd forgotten all about the endless days pursuing the traitors.

He'd located the mother lode.

Fake IDs, lists of addresses, and several papers written in code that would have to be deciphered. There were also three laptop computers that the tech wizards could use to gain information.

Talon had gathered it all, including the two male Pantera, before heading home.

Now he just wanted to return to his rooms at the communal Hunter house and collapse.

Giving the chains he held in his hands a tug, he moved through the thick undergrowth, not bothering to glance over his shoulder at the men who were leashed by heavy collars laced with malachite.

They'd given in to the inevitable without a fight, barely speaking on the trip back to the bayou.

That was fine with Talon.

If the Pantera didn't need the information the bastards could provide on why they'd become traitors and who was ultimately responsible for trying to destroy the Wildlands, he'd have happily killed them and left them to rot in Baton Rouge.

To him, loyalty and honor meant everything.

How could you call yourself a Pantera if you weren't willing to put the welfare of your people ahead of your own, selfish needs?

They'd reached a narrow canal choked with water lilies when Talon came to a sharp halt. His brows, the same shade of dark gold threaded with copper highlights as his hair, snapped together over his eyes that were a pale gold rimmed with jade.

He could sense a large number of Pantera rushing in his direction.

Never a good thing.

Tightening his grip on the chains, Talon was preparing for an attempt to rescue the traitors when a familiar cat the color of rich caramel with glowing gold eyes leaped gracefully over the canal to land directly at his side.

Instantly he relaxed.

Raphael, the leader of the Suits, had been like a father to Talon after the death of his parents in an airplane crash thirty years ago. Despite the fact that they were only distantly related, and Talon's faction was Hunters, not Diplomats, Raphael had been the one to visit the school where Talon was being trained in his duties. Whether it was to cheer him on during his athletic competitions or to kick his ass when he'd snuck into the nearby town, La Pierre, and left an alligator in the mayor's bathtub.

Raphael had also been the one to take him to The Cougar's Den and get him cross-eyed drunk when the cute little female he'd been chasing decided to dump him for another male.

Talon trusted this man above anyone else in the world.

There was a shimmering swirl of color before Raphael shifted into his human form, dressed like Talon in faded jeans and T-shirt.

A tall man with chiseled muscles, Raphael had a golden beauty that had driven females wild. At least until he'd stunned them all by arriving back at the Wildlands with a mate who was already carrying his young.

It was a miracle.

As long as they could keep Ashe and her baby alive.

Which was why Talon had been sent to track down the traitors.

"Welcome home, Talon," Raphael murmured, his lean face too pale and his golden eyes shadowed with the brutal fear that was threatening to destroy him.

"Why the welcome committee?" Talon demanded.

"We need to speak." Raphael's tone was flat. A sure sign his emotions were on the edge of a meltdown. He snapped his fingers and Sebastian appeared at his side. The Suit was a bronze-skinned male with glowing hazel eyes and a chiseled body that proved he didn't spend much time sitting behind a desk. His tawny hair was threaded with gold and brushed his broad shoulders. "Take the prisoners to the elders."

Talon tossed the chains toward Sebastian who curled his lips to growl at the cringing prisoners. Next, Talon shoved the backpack that held the computers and file folders into the Suit's hand.

"These need to go to Xavier," he said, referring to the brilliant head of the Geeks. If anyone could coax information out of the computers it would be Xavier.

Sebastian gave an unnecessary jerk on the chains, leading the prisoners away just as Raphael nodded his head toward a thick grove of cypress trees.

"This way," the Suit commanded.

Following in Raphael's wake, Talon studied the tense set of the older man's shoulders and the manner in which he turned his head from side to side, as if searching for hidden enemies.

"This speaking doesn't involve dungeons and chains, does it?" Talon muttered, not entirely joking.

Raphael sent a puzzled glance over his shoulder. "We don't have dungeons."

Talon grimaced, shoving his way past the veil of Spanish moss to step into the small clearing in the center of the trees.

"We didn't when I left, but things are clearly changing," he pointed out in dry tones.

"Unfortunately," Raphael agreed, restlessly pacing over the spongy ground.

Talon rolled his weary shoulders, sensing he wasn't going to see his bed anytime soon. "What did I miss?"

Raphael turned to meet his worried gaze. "You were already on the hunt when Jean-Baptiste returned with the female voodoun."

Talon nodded. He'd known the male Healer had gone to fetch the human female, but he'd been headed out of the Wildlands before Jean-Baptiste returned.

"Did she help Ashe?"

"I believe so."

"Thank the goddess," Talon breathed, relief shuddering through him.

Raphael's mate carried the future of the Pantera within her fragile womb. The knowledge that they'd allowed their enemies close enough to put her and the babe in danger laid heavily on all of them.

"Don't give thanks yet," Raphael warned.

"Why?"

The leader of the Suits scrubbed his hands over his face. Talon wondered when he'd last slept.

Probably not since Ashe had been attacked and infected with some potent toxin.

"I need to start at the beginning," Raphael growled.

"Here." Talon pulled out his silver flask filled with Don Julio tequila and tossed it toward his friend. "Tell me."

Raphael took a drink, grimacing as the expensive tequila slid down his throat. "As I said, Jean-Baptiste brought Isi to the Wildlands." Another grimace. "Much against her will."

Talon arched a brow. "She's prejudiced against the Pantera?"

"No. For some reason the Wildlands make her ill."

The Wildlands making someone ill? That was weird.

"I've never heard of that before," Talon said. "Of course, I don't have enough interest in humans to know what makes them sick."

"None of us have."

Talon shrugged. He didn't really care if she was sick or not. Nothing mattered but Ashe and the baby.

"Did she have a potion for Ashe?"

Raphael turned to glance at the heavy layers of moss that kept them hidden from the rest of the swamp, sending a chill of fear down Talon's spine.

Was he afraid someone was trying to spy on them?

Were there more traitors?

Shit.

"Actually her mere presence seems to give Ashe strength," he at last said, his voice low.

Okay. That seemed a good thing.

So why wasn't Raphael happier?

"I don't understand," Talon admitted.

Raphael returned to his pacing. "The Healers suspect that the toxin in Ashe's blood is targeted to attack the babe. It's taking every ounce of her strength to protect her child."

"That makes sense," Talon said. He'd already heard the poison was manifesting itself like a possession, with an intelligent design to destroy the baby. "What does the female have to do with it?"

"Having her near appears to…" Raphael searched for the word to describe the female's effect on his mate. "Steady Ashe."

"Steady?"

"It's almost as if she gives Ashe more strength."

Talon frowned. He didn't doubt the power of the voodoun. The spiritual world was a powerful force. But he'd always thought they needed potions and spells and rituals to weave their magic.

"She helps by being in the same room?" he demanded.

"She helps just being in the Wildlands."

Talon shook his head. He didn't like the thought that the female could somehow tamper with Ashe by her mere presence.

It was one thing to stir up a potion. Or even do one of those mysterious rituals they seemed to love.

But this…it was strange.

And he didn't trust strange.

"Do the Healers know why?"

Raphael's expression tightened, his eyes glowing gold with the power of his cat. "They're divided."

"Why do I sense I'm not going to like this?"

"Because you won't," Raphael said bluntly, halting his pacing to meet Talon's wary gaze. "Isi is Ashe's sister."

Talon blinked, his brain struggling to process the words.

"Sister?"

"Her *twin* sister."

Twin sister. God almighty.

"I thought you said Ashe's only relative was a drunkard mother," Talon said.

"That's what Ashe had always been told."

Talon narrowed his gaze, his vague unease solidifying into ruthless suspicion.

"And now this Isi claims to be her long-lost sister?"

Raphael shook his head. "No. The DNA revealed their connection."

The scientific proof of the two women's biological connection did nothing to ease Talon's distrust. Hell, it only made him more skeptical.

"That's one hell of a coincidence," he muttered.

"Yeah, that was my thought." Raphael shoved his fingers through his hair. "And it gets worse."

Talon rolled his eyes. When were things *not* getting worse?

"Great."

"The elders are convinced that Isi is some prophesied agent of doom."

Talon made a sound of disbelief at the cheesy, sci-fi description. He might even have laughed if it hadn't been for Raphael's grim expression. He had a feeling a laugh would earn him an ass-kicking even worse than the time he'd set up a moonshine still in the caves and sold the potent liquor to his classmates. How was he supposed to know he'd brewed the alcohol so pure it would make them sicker than dogs?

"Now you're just screwing with me," he instead growled.

"I wish I was," Raphael muttered. "The elders claim that Isi and Ashe's father was the Pantera Shaman."

It took a minute for Talon to recall the human who had once been called on by the elders to reveal the faction of an unborn Pantera. There were also rumors he'd had visions of the future.

It'd been years since Talon had last seen him.

He at last managed to dig the name from his memories.

"Chayton?"

"Yes."

"Didn't he die?"

Raphael grimaced. "The elders assumed he had."

Talon made a sound of disbelief. The elders rarely made mistakes.

Or maybe they just never admitted to them.

"Go on," he urged.

"They said that Chayton had a vision that his first born child would destroy the Wildlands," Raphael said, a hint of pity in his voice for the man who must have been devastated to reveal that his own daughter was born to be a force for evil.

Talon was far less sympathetic. He wasn't a firm believer in prophecies. There were too many ways they could be interpreted to offer a blueprint for the future.

But if the first born child was a danger to his people, he damned well intended to stop her.

"Isi was the first born?"

Raphael gave a sharp nod. "After the vision, Chayton took his pregnant wife and fled to the north of

21

the state. The babes were just being born when the elders tracked them down."

"They intended to sacrifice the child." The words were a statement, not a question.

The elders weren't the sort of females to wait and see if something might become a problem. They were firm believers in preemptive strikes.

"They did, but Chayton managed to distract them long enough to slip away," Raphael revealed. "The Hunters found traces of blood and a baby blanket, but no sign of the Shaman. When Dixie returned to La Pierre with Ashe the Elders kept a close guard on Dixie expecting Chayton to try and contact her if he remained alive. When the years passed with no word from the Shaman the Elders assumed he and the babe had died."

The Shaman had to have been extremely talented or extremely lucky to have escaped the elders for so long.

"Ashe knew nothing about her father?" he asked.

"No." Raphael narrowed his gaze, as if daring the younger man to call his mate a liar. Yeah. Talon was more likely to stick his head in the mouth of a gator. "The elders obviously tampered with Dixie's mind, forcing her to believe she only had one child and that her husband abandoned her."

Talon shuddered. Mind alterations on such a large scale could be extremely destructive to humans.

"Maybe it's not so surprising she turned to booze," he said. "What was the elders' response to Isi's arrival?"

"Cataclysmic." The lean features tightened. No doubt Raphael had been at the epicenter of that cataclysmic response. "They arrived at Ashe's room once the DNA results revealed her connection to Isi. Until that point they'd assumed that Isi's only threat was her connection to her voodoo shop."

Talon wasn't expecting that.

"They knew about her?"

"They've been keeping a careful watch on artists who specialize in tattoos with malachite."

Ah. Talon had to admit it was a reasonable precaution. The mineral was used to ground a cat inside a Pantera's body. Or for Nurturer therapists to soothe patients who couldn't control their minds or their cats. And, of course, the elders used it as punishment to cage a Pantera.

"Only a person with intimate knowledge of our cats would understand the magical properties of the mineral," he pointed out.

"There's also this."

Reaching into his pocket, Raphael pulled out his phone and flicked through the photos. Finding the one he was searching for, he turned the phone so Talon could see the image.

Talon leaned forward, easily determining the picture had been taken on the streets of New Orleans. It appeared to be a small store. The sort you could find in any narrow street or alleyway. The only thing to make it stand out was the blood-red shingle that read, THE CARE AND FEEDING OF VOODOO.

"I assume this is Isi's shop?" he demanded, not entirely sure what he was supposed to be seeing.

"Yes. And this is her vehicle."

Raphael zoomed the photo until Talon could see the white van parked in front of the store, the emblem of a spread-winged raven flying across a full moon painted on the side.

A low growl trickled from Talon's throat at the unmistakable Mark of Shakpi.

"Shit." He glanced up at Raphael's bleak face. "Do they intend to kill her?"

The golden eyes glowed with a dangerous determination. "Not as long as I keep them away."

Talon frowned. Raphael was usually the levelheaded one. The one who looked at every situation with a cool logic that was as annoying as hell.

Now, Talon couldn't help but worry that his friend was allowing his devotion to his mate to blind him to the potential danger of having Isi so near.

"Look, Raphael, I get that she's related to your mate, but if she's one of our enemies—"

"I don't give a shit if she's related or not," Raphael sharply interrupted. "Her presence is helping Ashe fight back the toxin."

Talon chose his words with care. Raphael was on the edge of snapping. He didn't want to be the one to tip him into a homicidal rage.

Not when he was standing only a few feet away.

"You're sure it's not some trick?"

"I'm not sure of anything." Raphael gave a low growl of frustration. "But know this, I'll do whatever is necessary to protect my mate and child."

Talon swallowed the words of warning that trembled on his lips.

They were a waste of breath as long as Raphael truly believed Isi was able to help his family.

"As we all will," he instead muttered, his tone grudging.

The golden gaze narrowed, the air prickling with the heat of Raphael's cat. "I hope you mean that."

"Why?"

"I have placed Isi under my protection, but I don't trust the elders," the older man bluntly confessed. "They're convinced she's the doom of the Pantera. They'll kill her if they get the opportunity."

That didn't seem like a bad plan to Talon. With Isi dead, then they could return to finding a less risky way to protect Ashe and the babe.

But his loyalty belonged to Raphael.

There was nothing he wouldn't do for the leader of the Suits.

"What do you want from me?" he asked.

"We haven't been able to do more than moderate Isi's illness."

Talon grimaced. "The Wildlands are probably trying to drive her out."

"It doesn't matter." Raphael waved a dismissive hand. "We had to move her to your parents' home."

Talon flinched, his eyes widening.

The pretty cottage that was hidden on the edge of the deepest marshes had been shut up the day that they received the news that Talon's parents had been killed in an airplane crash. Talon had moved to the Hunter house, and while he visited the cottage to perform the necessary upkeep, no one had actually stayed there for years.

He didn't keep it as some tragic temple to his dead parents. Or at least, not intentionally.

But he sure the hell didn't use it as a B&B for the potential doom of his people.

"You put her where?" he rasped, unable to believe that Raphael could be so insensitive.

Raphael met his accusing glare with a stubborn expression. He wasn't backing down.

"It's the most easily defended location," he pointed out, referring to the marshland that was deep and thick enough to keep out all but the most determined predators. "Besides, there's something in the house that eases her sickness."

Talon didn't care if it made her sprout wings and a halo.

"You're asking a lot, *mon ami*."

Raphael shoved his phone into his pocket and folded his arms over his chest. He'd lost weight in the past month, but he was still big, tough and capable of twisting Talon into a painful knot.

"I'm not done," he warned.

Talon counted to ten.

"What?"

"I expect you to become her guardian."

Talon made a sound of shock. "Say that again."

The golden eyes narrowed. "You heard me."

He had. Unfortunately.

"Why me?"

"I trust you."

The words struck straight at his heart, and Talon threw his hands up in defeat.

"Fuck."

CHAPTER TWO

For the first time in weeks, Isi felt warm. Not just 'wrapped in heavy blankets until she was nearly smothered' warm. But warm from the inside out.

And even better, the constant sense of nausea was gone.

Completely, utterly gone.

With a sigh she snuggled closer to the source of the warmth, breathing deeply of the intoxicating musk that was driving away the hideous illness that plagued her at varying levels of hell since she arrived in the Wildlands.

She didn't know what was creating the delicious scent, and she didn't really care.

She just wanted to wrap herself in the soothing sensations.

As if answering her prayer, a warm hand slid down her back, cupping her ass.

"Oh, thank god," she groaned as the touch sent heat rushing through her veins. "Don't stop. That feels so good."

"I haven't even started, darling," a rough male voice whispered in her ear.

Isi was jerked out of her lovely dream, belatedly realizing she was no longer alone. What the hell? She forced open her heavy lids, her breath squeezed from her lungs as she encountered a pair of glowing golden eyes rimmed in jade.

They were spectacular eyes.

Clear, cunning and lethally male.

And they were set in a face that was drop-dead, do-me-now gorgeous.

Wide brow, a narrow blade of a nose, high cheekbones and sensually carved lips.

A true masterpiece of DNA.

Still foggy from sleep, Isi felt a surge of female appreciation tingle down her spine.

That was the kind of face that made smart women do stupid things.

And enjoy every second of it.

A dark, enticing arousal stirred deep inside her, shocking Isi with the intensity of her response.

She might enjoy the sight of a handsome man in a purely artistic way, but she didn't immediately consider how quickly she could rip off his clothes and wrap herself around him.

It was at last the inhuman glow in his eyes that snapped her out of her growing obsession.

Oh, shit.

This wasn't a man.

He was Pantera.

And he was currently rolling until he was perched on top of her.

"Hello, darling," he drawled, his lips curling as he watched her expression tighten with a surge of angry suspicion. "If I'd known you were waiting in my bed I would have returned sooner."

She shoved her hands against his chest, not surprised when he refused to budge. Even through the thin blanket she could feel his lean body honed to sleek, chiseled muscles. The shove was just a distraction so she could knee him in the nuts.

It didn't matter how tough a man was, he had one glaring vulnerability.

With a well-practiced jerk of her leg, she aimed directly between his legs. "Get off me, you pervert."

There was a low snarl as the cat managed to block her debilitating strike, using his longer legs to pin her to the mattress.

"No need to play rough, darling." His tongue traced the shell of her ear, sending unwelcome jolts of bliss straight to her pussy. "Unless that's the way you like it."

She hissed in frustration, trying to deny the fact that her entire body was humming with a treacherous awareness.

God dammit. When a man held her against her will it was a reason for homicide.

Not melting into a shivering mess of aching hunger.

"If I was playing rough I'd already have kicked the hair off your balls," she muttered.

"My balls aren't hairy." He nipped the lobe of her ear, grabbing her hand to lower it toward the hardening length of his cock. "Do you need proof?"

"Hell no." She wrenched her hand free, punching him in the chest with a force that would have broken the rib of a human. "Who are you?"

"Your reluctant host."

"Host?" Isi scowled. Raphael had told her that the pretty cottage hadn't been used for years. Of course, he'd also told her she wasn't a prisoner, but every time she tried to leave he warned her that the mysterious elders were just waiting for an opportunity to kill her. After a month of being stuck in the bayou with a bunch of angry cats who considered her the enemy, she was reaching her limit. In fact, tonight might very well have tipped her over the edge. "This is your house?"

"It's my parents' home, but this is my bed," the male Pantera said. "Why did you choose it?"

"What?"

"There are four bedrooms." He studied her with an unnerving intensity. Even in the darkness she knew what he was seeing. Short, jet black hair with blue streaks, mussed from sleep. A pale face with delicate features that were dominated by a pair of eyes so dark they looked black. His gaze lowered to the tattoo of a rose wrapped around a candle that ran from below her right ear down to her shoulder, before lingering on the diamond piercing in each nostril. His expression remained unreadable, but there was no missing the thickening of the intoxicating musk that filled the air. "Why did you choose mine?"

Isi hesitated. There was no way in hell she was going to admit she'd been drawn to the room because it'd eased the sickness that was a constant companion.

Not when an awful, unbearable suspicion was beginning to form in the back of her mind.

"It had the best view," she at last muttered.

His lips brushed a searing path of temptation down her throat. "Liar."

Her heart slammed against her ribs and her pussy clenched in brutal need as his lips teased the pulse at the base of her neck.

Oh...hell.

Without warning, she was suddenly slamming her fists against his chest, desperately trying to wriggle from beneath his hard body. There was no way to disguise her stupid arousal from the man's freakishly sensitive senses, but she'd be damned if she'd lie there like an obedient doll.

"Get. Off."

Lifting his head, the man frowned in confusion as he tried to halt her attack without hurting her. "Settle down, female."

"Not until you release me."

He hissed as she raked her nails down his face, rolling to the side so she could scramble off the bed.

"Damn wildcat," he muttered, his gaze running a brooding path down her slender body covered by a pair of silk shorts and camisole top.

Instinctively she folded her arms over her breasts, more to hide the hardened points of her nipples than out of any sort of modesty.

Young girls raised in orphanages didn't have the privilege of being bashful.

"Tell me your name," she commanded.

He continued to sprawl across the heavy four-poster bed that matched the hand-carved furniture that filled the second story room. He should have looked ridiculous in the cozy setting with handwoven rugs, walls lined with stuffed bookcases, and the echoes of a loving childhood, but he didn't.

He looked…at home.

A familiar pang of envy sliced through her heart before she was squashing the worthless regret.

Homes were places you kept your shit until you moved on to the next place. End of story.

"Talon," he said, his voice rubbing over her skin like rough silk.

Isi frowned. She had a vague memory of Ashe mentioning the Hunter who had been tracking down Pantera traitors.

"No one told me you lived here." She edged her way toward the door. She needed to be away from the disturbing cat. Far, far away. "I'll go somewhere else."

"Where?"

"Home." She didn't know what she was going to say until the word left her lips, but suddenly she knew that's exactly where she was going. She'd had enough of freaking Pantera and their soggy Wildlands. She belonged in New Orleans, running her shop. "Where I should have gone weeks ago."

"What about your sister?"

She shrugged, continuing to inch toward the door. "I can come back."

With a blur of motion, Talon was off the bed and blocking her path. "No."

Her jaw clenched as she was forced to come to a halt. "No?"

He planted his fists on his hips, the T-shirt stretched tight over the sculpted muscles of his chest.

"Raphael sent me here to protect you." He didn't bother to hide his anger at being stuck on babysitting duty. "I can't do that if you leave the Wildlands."

Her chin tilted. "Thanks, fur ball, but I've been taking care of myself a long time."

The golden eyes narrowed. "What is it with you and my fur?"

"I want it staying the hell away from me."

He prowled forward, his heat wrapping around her with sensuous pleasure. "You weren't so averse to me and my fur when you were clinging to me and telling me how good it felt."

She meant to hold her ground. She really did. But as he continued his ruthless path forward, she discovered herself retreating until her back was pressed against a tall bookcase.

Annoying ass.

"That was—"

He halted inches away, his hands lifting to grip the shelf on each side of her head. "What?"

"I was suddenly feeling better, that's all."

"Raphael mentioned it has something to do with the house," he said, his gaze lowering to the pulse that thundered at the base of her throat.

Isi grimaced. Yeah. She'd thought it was the house.

Until Talon appeared and the illness went from manageable to completely gone.

"Whatever," she muttered. "I'll feel even better at my own house."

He leaned down, his breath searing over her lips like a kiss. "Ain't. Gonna. Happen."

33

"It's not your decision."

"Do you think you would last one second without Raphael's protection?"

"So he keeps telling me." Her lips flattened with a stubborn determination. She'd allowed herself to be bullied into staying for weeks. Or at least she told herself she'd been bullied. Otherwise she would have to admit that she stayed for Ashe. An unacceptable explanation. "How do I know that's not just bullshit to keep me here?"

"Raphael doesn't have to use empty threats," Talon warned. "If he decides to keep you here, I guarantee you that you'll stay. One way or another."

She glared into the savagely beautiful face. "So when you said you're here to guard me, you meant I'm your prisoner."

"Raphael asked me to make sure you continued to help to his mate."

Oh, yes. Raphael had made it clear that he would move heaven and earth to protect his mate and child.

Which didn't make her jealous at all. Nope. Not at all.

"And what I want doesn't matter?" she snapped.

"No."

She gave a humorless laugh at his complete lack of apology. "Nice. "

"It's the way it is."

"Fine." She dipped down to slip under his arm, heading toward the door. "I'm too tired to argue."

"Where are you going?" he demanded, once again moving to stand in her way.

"To another room."

"Why?" He had the balls to reach out and lightly grasp her chin, turning her head toward the bed dominating the room. "This bed is all toasty warm."

"You said this was your room."

His thumb brushed her lower lips, his touch sending a rush of arousal through her. "I'll share."

Her mouth went dry as the vivid image of being spread naked across the mattress as this man kissed a path from the top of her blue-streaked hair to the tips of her fuchsia-painted toes blazed through her mind.

Desire streaked through her, white hot and so fierce it made her knees week.

God, she had to get out of there.

"In your dreams," she said, the words sounding lame even to her.

His gaze followed his thumb as it traced the stubborn line of her jaw.

"We're stuck here together," he murmured, his voice husky with invitation. "We might as well enjoy our time."

She slapped away his hand before stepping around his body and heading toward the door with a grim determination.

Dammit.

She didn't know what was wrong with her.

The man was a damned cat. And worse, he considered her nothing more than an unwelcome duty.

"I'd rather sleep with a snake," she informed him, her head held high.

He waited until she was at the door before he called out to her. "Isi."

Reluctantly she glanced over her shoulder, refusing to acknowledge the impact of his golden beauty as he stood in a pool of moonlight.

"What?"

His eyes narrowed. "Raphael might need you for now, but I don't trust you an inch." His soft words sliced through her like a dagger. "Don't give me a reason to kill you."

She stormed from the room and down the hall, choosing the bedroom furthest away before slamming the door behind her.

The arrogant son of a bitch.

How dare he threaten to kill her after…

After what?

She gave a choked laugh, pressing a hand to her lips as the faint queasiness began to return.

After he'd offered to have sex with her?

No. It wasn't even sex.

It was a quick fuck with a stranger.

It was clearly time she returned to her own life.

Far away from the bayous and Pantera males who would be greatly improved by having their bloated heads stuffed and mounted over the nearest fireplace.

***

A thrill of excitement raced through Talon as he slid silently through the underbrush. In his cat form he moved with a silent grace that made certain his prey was unaware she was being hunted.

Isi.

His excitement turned to a darker, more enticing emotion as he caught the scent of magnolia.

The female wasn't at all what he'd been expecting.

Harbingers of doom shouldn't look like exotic butterflies, with raven black hair highlighted with brilliant blue, and black eyes that contrasted with pale, milky skin. Even the tattoo and piercings that should have made her look hard only emphasized her striking beauty.

A rare, exquisite creature that had made lust explode through him from the second he'd caught sight of her curled in his bed.

Of course, she did have the attitude, he wryly acknowledged.

But even the sharp tongue and don't-screw-with-me insolence fascinated him.

It made him want to break through the brittle facade to find the warm, passionate woman beneath.

And she would be passionate.

He'd caught the scent of her arousal. An arousal that matched his own.

She wanted him. Just like he wanted her.

Beneath him.

Now.

Realizing they were nearing the border of the Wildlands, Talon began to close the distance.

He'd heard her the second Isi had left her room to creep downstairs. She'd taken time to slip into the laundry room and grab one of the sweat suits that every Pantera kept in his home. Even though their clothing usually transformed during the shift, there were times when they were stressed, or injured, or too weary to maintain full control of their transformation. The sweats were bought in bulk to be disposable.

Then, she'd slipped from his house like a thief in the night.

Talon had allowed her escape.

He wanted to know where the hell she was going and who she was meeting.

Now it was clear that she'd been serious when she'd said she intended to go home.

With a silent burst of speed, Talon was circling around her, hidden by the thick vegetation. He felt a brief flare of confusion when he caught sight of her pale face and the hand pressed to her lips as if she was struggling against the urge to vomit.

She was far sicker than she had been at his house.

And for some stupid reason the realization sent a stab of fury through his heart. As if the thought of her in distress was painful to him.

With a low growl he crushed the unwelcome suspicion, instead pouncing forward, concentrating on his shift from cat to human as he carefully knocked Isi to the mossy ground.

An explosion of magic burst through his body, making him shudder as his bones and muscle realigned.

An exhilarating sensation.

But not nearly so exhilarating as the feel of her slender curves pressed beneath him.

"Going somewhere, darling?" he drawled, running a searching gaze down her body to make certain she hadn't been hurt in the fall.

Not that he should care, he fiercely told himself.

He'd warned her what would happen if she tried to flee.

Still, he couldn't entirely shake his aggravating aversion to seeing her in pain.

Isi's eyes widened in fear before she realized exactly who was pinning her to the ground. Immediately her fear altered to pure fury.

"Shit." She wriggled beneath him, her face losing its pasty shade of green as his musk began to fill the air. "Stop leaping on top of me."

Sweet sparks of arousal tingled through his blood as she writhed against his swelling cock, the intensity of his pleasure wrenching a low growl from his throat.

Lowering his head, he pressed his nose to the curve of her throat, breathing deep of her magnolia scent.

"I wouldn't twitch a single muscle if I were you," he warned.

Her muscles tensed, her heart pounding so loud he could hear the frantic beats. "Why?"

"Because chasing you has turned me on." Unable to resist temptation, Talon sank his teeth into her silken flesh, not hard enough to draw blood, but enough to satisfy the cat inside him who abruptly wanted a taste of this female. Lust thundered through him. "Do you want to run some more?"

She slammed her fist against his back, her entire body trembling. But not with fear. Or anger.

"I just want you to leave me alone," she rasped.

"Liar." His voice thickened as the intoxicating scent of her cream teased at his senses. Her pussy was already wet and ready for him to penetrate. His cock twitched, anxious to fulfill her need. "I excite you."

Another blow to his back. "You're pissing me off, fur boy."

He licked a path down her throat, his cat prowling just below the surface, as if unnerved by the intoxicating flavor of her skin.

"Then why do you smell like sex?" he demanded.

"Because you're delusional," she muttered, making another bid for freedom.

"Dammit," he snarled, lifting his head to glare into her wide eyes. It was one thing to taunt her with his awareness of her arousal. It was another to realize that he was perilously close to ripping off her clothes and fucking her right there. He might be a Pantera, but he wasn't an animal. "I told you to stay still."

"I don't take orders from you..." Her words trailed away as he pressed a hand to her forehead, his gaze searching her pale face. "What are you doing?"

"You were sick," he said in abrupt tones, temporarily distracted from his potent lust.

She frowned. "This whole place makes me sick."

"Now you're better."

Something flickered in her eyes. Something she was trying to hide from him.

"We're close to border."

"No." He gave a slow shake of his head. "You were better in my home. And now you're better because I'm holding you," he reasoned out loud. Then the truth struck him. "It's me," he said, watching as the flush of color stained her cheeks. "I make you better."

She glared at him in frustration. "God, could your ego get any bigger?"

He leaned down to nip the tip of her nose. "Admit it."

"No."

"Why not?" His lips twisted as his lust returned in full, painful force. Christ, his cock was pressing so hard against the zipper of his jeans he was afraid it might bust through. "I'll admit your scent is driving me out of my fucking mind."

"Talon."

He hissed, heat exploding through him as he allowed his lips to trail over her cheek to the edge of her mouth.

"Say it again," he urged.

She trembled, her hands spread against his back as she forgot to fight him. "What?"

"My name." He used his tongue to trace the lush temptation of her lower lip. "Say it again."

"Talon."

"I like to hear it on your lips," he said, kissing the line of her jaw before heading down the silken skin of her throat.

Her nails bit into his shoulders as she arched in pleasure beneath him. "What are you doing to me?"

"Darling, I'll do anything you want," he muttered, forgetting where they were and, more importantly, who she was.

Nothing mattered but the sharp-edged hunger that clawed at him whenever he was close to this female.

He reached the neckline of her sweatshirt, impatiently using his chin to push it aside so he could trace her collarbone with his lips.

"Oh," she breathed, rubbing against the thick thrust of his erection.

He growled, about to reach down and yank off the loose bottom of her sweats when his gaze caught sight of a tiny mark at the bottom of her collarbone.

It was like being doused in icy-cold water.

One second all he could think about was the savage need that was pounding through his body, and the next he was pushing himself upright and shoving shaking hands through his tousled hair.

"Shit," he rasped.

She raised herself onto her elbows. "What?"

His gaze remained glued to the birthmark that marred the perfect ivory of her skin. "A raven."

She flinched. As if he'd physically struck her.

"It's not a raven, it's a birthmark."

"The symbol of evil." The words left his lips before he could consider their impact on Isi.

Hell, he was a Hunter, not a Suit.

"Evil?" Isi surged to her feet, grabbing a hefty stick off the ground to swing toward his head with a magnificent fury. "Get out of here, you son of a bitch."

Angry with himself for having forgotten he intended to treat this female as the enemy, and potentially putting his people in danger, he turned to walk away.

He needed some distance to pull his head out of his ass and start thinking clearly.

Or at least try to ease his raging hard-on.

"Gladly," he snarled, headed back to his parents' cottage.

The branch went whizzing past his head, grazing his ear. "And stay the hell away," she shouted.

Turning his head, he sent her a last glare. "You leave the Wildlands and the elders will kill you. Make no mistake about it," he growled.

She flipped him off. "Bastard."

Talon stormed away.

For the first time he felt like a bastard.

CHAPTER THREE

Isi woke with a weary groan to find the late morning sun pouring through her open window.

Momentarily disoriented, she pushed herself to a sitting position, glancing in confusion around the room painted a cheery yellow.

What the hell? This wasn't the room she'd been using for the past month.

It took a minute before the memories from the night before slammed into her.

Talon.

The bastard.

Talon the Bastard. Yep. That suited him to perfection.

Shoving herself out of the bed, she stomped her way to the attached bathroom.

Last night she'd hovered at the edge of the Wildlands for over an hour before the sickness had driven her back to the cottage. Her every instinct had warned her to return to New Orleans and take the first bus the hell out of town, but she wasn't entirely sure that the threat of the elders wasn't real.

Finally she'd had no choice but to return to the cottage where there was some measure of relief from the constant sickness.

Although not as much as there had been during the night, she realized as she quickly showered and pulled on a robe. Which could only mean that Talon was no longer in the cottage.

Good, she savagely told herself, entering the room he'd taken over, to gather her clothes and take them to her new, painfully sunny room. She'd rather be sick than have to endure his repulsive company.

Pretending she actually did find him repulsive, Isi pulled on a pair of jeans and skimpy top that hit just below the gentle swell of her breasts. She smiled with a grim defiance as she realized the top was cut low enough to display her evil birthmark. Then, spiking her blue-streaked hair, she headed out the door and to the clinic where her sister continued to fight for her life.

Acutely aware of the cats who trailed behind her at a discreet distance, she followed the narrow path that led from the isolated marsh to the village, keeping her head high.

She'd learned from day one that her presence in the Wildlands attracted unwelcome attention.

Some curious, some hopeful, but most filled with a predatory hunger that assured her they were just waiting for the opportunity to rip her to shreds.

Not the nicest neighbors a girl could have, but sadly they weren't the worst.

She'd run away from the orphanage when she was barely fourteen to live on the streets of Chicago.

Tough to top that.

Reaching the clinic, she entered the wooden structure through a side door and headed directly to her sister's room at the back of the building.

Unlike human hospitals, there was no stench of antiseptic or disinfectant. Instead the air was laced with the scent of healing plants and potions as well as the exotic musk that was unique to each Pantera.

There was also a decided lack of sterile white walls and linoleum floors. In this clinic the walls were paneled in rich cherry wood with floors covered by handwoven rugs.

Pushing open the door to her sister's room, she stepped inside, not surprised to find Raphael sitting beside the bed.

The male refused to leave his mate's side unless it was a matter of dire urgency.

Rising to his feet at Isi's entrance, Raphael motioned for her to take his seat beside the bed.

"Good morning, Isi."

She hurriedly perched on the edge of the chair, always a little on edge around the man.

He might have sworn to protect her, but he was clearly ready to snap. She didn't want to be around if something happened to Ashe.

"How is she?" Isi asked, focusing on the dark-haired woman lying in the wooden bed, covered by a hand-stitched quilt.

"She's holding her own," Raphael said, the weariness in his voice drawing her gaze to his haggard features.

Christ, he looked like he hadn't slept in days.

"Why don't you go rest?" she offered. "I'll sit with Ashe."

There was a brief hesitation, as if he was debating whether or not to trust Isi alone with his beloved mate. Then, obviously realizing he was near collapse, he gave a reluctant nod.

"I'll be just down the hall."

The Pantera leaned down to place a gentle kiss on his mate's lips before turning to leave the room and gently closing the door behind him.

Alone with the female they claimed was her sister, Isi studied the pale, perfect features that held only a faint resemblance to her own. Over the past month she spent a part of each day with Ashe, usually watching her sleep, although there were times when the other woman would wake long enough for a short conversation.

Still, Ashe remained more a stranger than a member of her family.

Which suited Isi just fine.

Concentrating on her sister with a fierce intensity that didn't allow any stray thoughts of *Talon the Bastard*, she was aware the second Ashe's lashes twitched and her hand unconsciously reached for her mate.

"Raphael?"

Isi leaned forward, lightly grasping the outstretched hand. "It's Isi."

The thick lashes lifted to reveal beautiful brown eyes. "Sister."

Isi stretched her lips into an uncomfortable smile. "That's what they tell me."

Ashe gave Isi's fingers a squeeze. "I always wanted a sister. Didn't you?"

Isi hid her shudder.

When she was young she'd learned that the only way to stay alive was to stay on the move and avoid attention. Something that would be impossible with family or friends.

Having a sister was a burden she couldn't afford.

Still, Ashe was studying her with her big, hopeful eyes. It would feel like kicking a puppy to admit the truth.

"I…" She struggled for words that would offer comfort without being an outright lie. "Wanted not to be alone."

"Yes." Ashe gave a weak nod of her head, looking impossibly beautiful despite the pallor of her skin and the shadows beneath her eyes. "I've always been alone. Until Raphael."

Isi frowned, perplexed by the soft words. "I thought you lived with our mother?"

Ashe wrinkled her nose. "Dixie wasn't much of a mother. She spent most of her time and money at the local bar." She hesitated before asking the question that had obviously been on her mind. "What about our father?"

Isi stiffened. "What about him?"

"Did you know him?"

"No." Isi felt a familiar stab of rage toward the man who had abandoned her when she needed him the most. "He dumped me at an orphanage in Shreveport and disappeared."

"Did you ever search for him?"

Isi scowled. Like she'd waste one precious second of her life on the worthless sperm donor who'd impregnated their mother?

"Why should I?" she demanded. "If he wanted to be with me he wouldn't have tossed me away like a piece of trash."

Ashe placed a hand on her swelling stomach, the gesture revealing her instinctive urge to protect the child growing so rapidly in her womb.

"Now you know he had no choice."

Isi abruptly released her sister's hand and rose to her feet. She'd done her best to pretend the elders' claim of her birth was nothing more than a fairy tale.

And she'd been remarkably successful.

Of course, she had a lot of practice at pretending the nasty things in her life didn't exist.

"Do I?" she muttered.

"You don't believe the elders?" Ashe asked.

Isi moved to gaze at out the window that offered a view of the clearing where the Pantera gathered for their meals.

There was no denying it was a beautiful sight, even for a girl who'd never spent more than an hour away from the city.

The long tables covered in green cloth set among the lush flowers and cypress trees. The unexpected wooden statues that were tucked among the azaleas to provide charming glimpses of native art. The nearby lake that sparkled in the lazy sunlight.

It was a land crafted by magic.

A magic that was fading.

And they wanted to blame her.

"Would you, if you were me?" She gave a humorless laugh, her voice edged with a bitterness she couldn't hide. "You get to be the beautiful princess who saves the Pantera while I'm the evil twin who offers nothing but destruction."

She heard Ashe's soft gasp of remorse. "Isi, I'm sorry. I didn't think—"

"Look, it's not like I give a shit," Isi interrupted the soft words. Hell, the only thing worse than being tagged as some sort of Antichrist was pity. The mere hint gave her hives. "Only suckers believe in prophecies."

"You're not evil."

Hidden behind her well-perfected wall of indifference, she turned to meet her sister's sympathetic gaze.

"Well, I'm not good," she said. "And it doesn't bother me at all."

"I mean what I say," Ashe insisted, clearly as stubborn as Isi. She smiled wryly. At least they had one thing in common. "You're not evil."

"Great." Isi shrugged, just wanting to be done with painful conversation. "If you could convince the crazy cats in charge I'm one of the good guys, I'll be on my way back home."

Ashe reached out her hand, her expression filled with a wistful yearning that tugged perilously at Isi's heart.

"We'll figure this out," she promised. "Together."

Isi instinctively backed away. She wasn't ready to give Ashe what she so obviously desired.

A sister.

"Yeah. Whatever." She continued to back toward the door. "I have to go."

Ashe dropped her hand, her gaze searching Isi's face. "You look better."

Isi came to a reluctant halt. "I was. Now..." She swallowed her words. There was no way in hell she was going to admit that there was something about Talon that eased her illness. "It doesn't matter."

Ashe bit her lip, her lids already beginning to droop. "I'm worried I'm draining you of your strength and that's what is making you sick."

Isi shrugged. "Don't sweat it, I'm tough."

Her sister struggled against the rising tide of weariness. "Isi—"

"I'll come back after dinner."

Isi slipped from the room, but lingered until she was certain her sister was deeply asleep.

It wasn't that she cared whether or not Ashe might feel alone. Or need something before Raphael returned.

It was just...

With a muttered curse, Isi headed out of the clinic and straight to the cottage.

This entire place was making her nuts.

***

NEW ORLEANS

Talon ignored the closed sign clearly displayed on the door of the voodoo shop. He wasn't a man who let pesky barriers stand in his way when he wanted something. Still, he was civilized enough to use his lock-picking skills to deal with the door rather than just kicking the damned thing open.

Glancing up and down the narrow street, he slipped inside and shut the door behind him. There would be witnesses to his B & E, of course. The specialty shops that lined the streets weren't so busy that the proprietors weren't aware of what was going on in neighboring stores. He could only hope they'd wait to see if he tried to walk out with a bag of loot before they called the cops.

Halting just inside the door, Talon immediate realized he wasn't alone.

Despite the heavy scent of incense that hung in the air there was no missing the smell of two human males. Or the sour stench that marked them as enemies.

Walking past the rows of leather-bound books, crystals that came in every size and color, ceramic pots that were filled with Isi's potions, and voodoo dolls, Talon silently paced to the body art room at the back of the store.

He hesitated at the open doorway, scanning the brightly lit room for hidden danger.

There wasn't much to see. The walls were covered with a variety of tattoo patterns and framed pictures of happy customers. There were two narrow massage tables covered with white paper, and rolling cabinets that held the paraphernalia needed by the tattoo artists.

No hidden closets or cupboards.

And best of all…no exits.

Curling his nose at the strange odor that clung to those humans who carried the Mark of Shakpi, Talon turned his attention to the two men who had yet to notice his arrival.

Idiots.

One was seated at the end of a table. He was a young, blond-haired man with the hard muscles of a dedicated bodybuilder. He had a dozen tattoos running up his arms and around his thick neck, but he wasn't at the shop for another.

No. The second man who was standing in front of him was holding a small metal rod with a flat piece of metal at the end.

A branding iron.

And Talon would bet his left nut it had a raven design on it.

A stupid, sharp-edged disappointment sliced through him before he was sternly reminding himself that he'd come to Isi's shop precisely because the elders suspected Isi was connected to their enemies.

What else had he expected?

With a shake of his head he forced himself to concentrate on silently stepping into the room. The men might be mere humans, but Raphael had discovered that their enemies had weapons that could weaken a Pantera and make their cats dangerously vulnerable.

"Am I interrupting?"

With a flurry of curses both men jerked their gazes toward the doorway.

The blond on the table was the first to recover. "Hey, this is a private—"

53

"Fuck," the one with the branding iron breathed. He had lanky black hair, a narrow face that had a rat-like quality, and brown eyes the color of mud, but there was an intelligence in his gaze that was missing from his companion. "Run."

"I don't think so."

Talon stood in the doorway, bracing himself as the blond pulled a knife and charged forward. He waited until the man was in striking distance, grabbing the arm holding the knife and using the attacker's own momentum to his advantage as he spun and slammed him face first into the doorjamb.

Having momentarily stunned his opponent, Talon spoke directly into his ear.

"Drop the knife and sit in the corner like a good boy and you might make it out of here alive," he offered.

Possessing the tedious belief that his size made him the toughest guy in the room, the blond wrenched his arm free and swung the knife toward Talon's face.

"Fuck you."

Dodging the blade, Talon grabbed the man's bloated head and with one efficient twist broke his neck.

He'd given the moron a chance to live.

Allowing the dead man to drop to the floor, Talon turned his attention to the slender, rat-faced man clutching the branding iron as if it could protect him.

Talon stepped forward, a lethal smile curling his lips. "We need to chat."

"I don't know who the hell you are, but—"

"Don't lie," Talon overrode the arrogant bluff. "I've seen you with Raphael."

"Yes…" A cunning light glowed in the mud eyes. "Yes, that's right. I'm Derek and I spy for him. He's going to be pissed if you blow my cover."

With a blur of motion, Talon was standing directly in front of the man, the tip of his dagger beneath his chin.

"Here's the deal," he said in soft, lethal tones. "You've been working with Suits. I'm a Hunter. Do you know what that means?"

The man licked his lips. "No."

Talon allowed his cat to glow in his eyes, watching the man with a hunger that would terrify any human.

"It means that my job description is tracking down enemies and killing them." He allowed the dagger to pierce the man's skin. "I don't negotiate. I don't heal. I don't nurture. I kill. And I do it very, very well."

"Fine," the man hissed, his expression sullen. "What do you want?"

"Answers."

"To what?"

"Who do you work for?"

"Isi," he answered without hesitation. "She owns this joint."

Talon clenched his teeth, pretending his cat wasn't snarling in disbelief. What did his cat know about human treachery?

"She trained you to brand traitors with that mark?"

Something flickered in the mud eyes. A warning that he was about to lie.

"She—"

"The truth or I'll start cutting off body parts." He lowered the dagger to press it against the man's dick. There was nothing like threatening to take an idiot's manhood to put him in the mood to share. "Starting here."

A layer of sweat coated the man's face, but his expression remained defiant. "No. The bitch has no idea what's going on."

Talon's grip tightened on the handle of the dagger. Did he believe the man?

Actually…he did.

Derek might pretend to be a tough guy, but at his core he was a coward.

If he could try to throw blame on Isi to cover his own ass, he would.

Refusing to dwell on the surge of relief that rushed through him, Talon nodded toward the iron rod still held in Derek's hand.

"Then who gave you the brand?"

"I made it myself." He lifted it to reveal the raven on the bottom. "Like it?"

Rage blasted through Talon.

These son of a bitches were destroying his homeland.

His people.

He wanted answers. Then he wanted to rip the bastard into tiny, bloody strips.

"It's as offensive as you are," he snarled. "Where did you learn to create the symbol?"

The man licked his lips, no doubt sensing Talon was just waiting for an excuse to kill him.

"I was approached by a voodoo priestess while I was in jail for a minor disagreement with my ex-wife," he said.

Voodoo priestess would match what Vincent and Savoy had told Bayon.

"What was her name?"

The man shrugged. "I don't know."

Talon lifted the dagger to press it beneath Derek's chin.

"Don't screw with me," he growled.

The man hissed in pain, but he was smart enough not to try to pull away. "I'm serious. She called herself Lady Cerise, but when I tried to find her later no one had ever heard of her. She must have used a false name."

"What did she say to you?"

"She paid my bail and told me she had a job for me," Derek admitted. "She gave me a card with the symbol of the raven flying across a full moon, and the address. Then she left."

"What was the job?"

"I went to the address that was an old warehouse where I met a group of men who promised an endless supply of money if I did what I was told and didn't ask too many questions."

Talon narrowed his gaze. Even with the threat of death, he was surprised Derek would so easily answer his questions.

He'd sensed the man was a coward, but surely he had to worry his fellow traitors would discover he squealed?

"For doing what?"

The man glanced toward the branding iron clutched in his hand. "My primary job is to brand the new recruits, but I do whatever I'm told to do."

"How did you end up in this shop?" he demanded, needing to know his connection to Isi. Why? He scowled, refusing to answer the question. "Was it because of her birthmark?"

Derek blinked in genuine bafflement. "What birthmark?"

"Never mind," he growled, aggravated he'd even asked the question. "Why did you choose this shop?"

"It was Lon."

"Who?"

"The alpha dog of our little crew." Derek's lips curled in disdain. The loser clearly had an allergy to authority. Typical. "He wanted me here to keep an eye on Isi."

Talon slid the dagger toward the man's throat, his eyes glowing as his cat snarled for blood.

"Why?"

Derek stiffened, the stench of his fear making Talon grimace. Still, his expression remained insolent.

"Lon wanted to know where she was and who was visiting the shop."

"He wanted to know about the Pantera?"

"Lon wasn't specific. He wanted me to keep a log on everyone who entered the shop." The mud eyes darkened with frustration. "I assume they were hoping someone would contact her, but they didn't share the information with me. I was just an insignificant peon."

Talon studied Derek's rat face. "And that's it?"

He gave a lift of one shoulder. "For me."

"What about the others?"

"There are some who sneak into the Wildlands and perform some hokey ritual," Derek said, unaware of Talon's burst of fury. Those hokey rituals were destroying his home. "And others who spend most of their time traveling around the world."

"Recruiters?"

"No." Derek arched backward, as if trying to remove his chin from the sharp edge of Talon's blade. "Like I said, they're looking for someone."

Talon was instantly intrigued.

If his enemies wanted this person, then it was imperative the Pantera got their hands on him first.

"You have some idea who this person is? Man or woman? Human or Pantera?"

Bitter envy twisted the man's expression. "That info was above my pay grade."

Talon made a sound of impatience. "Where is the warehouse?"

Derek abruptly spit in Talon's face, using the momentary distraction to yank out the gun he'd had holstered at his lower back.

Talon belatedly realized why the man had been so eager to answer his questions. He'd simply been trying to keep Talon distracted long enough to get out his weapon.

"That's enough questions," the man roared. "Die, you fucking animal."

"Not today."

With a speed the human couldn't hope to match, Talon wrenched the gun from the man's hand, and with one swing of his arm he'd knocked Derek off his feet to crash head first into the wall.

The man landed heavily on the floor, blood flowing from the cut on his forehead. He was injured, but Talon could hear the steady beat of his heart.

Grimly he forced himself to turn and leave the room, closing the door behind him.

There was nothing he wanted more than to cut out the man's heart and feed it to the gators, but he was a Hunter who understood that sometimes the best way to catch his prey was to use bait.

Once Derek woke up, his first instinct would be to return to the Mother Ship.

Or in this case, the warehouse where Lon and his crew were hidden.

Talon intended to make sure the bastard was followed.

Pulling his phone out of his pocket, he hit speed dial. "I need a surveillance team in New Orleans. Oh, and there's a stiff to clean up."

CHAPTER FOUR

Isi was standing in the kitchen with pretty white cabinets and a black and white tiled floor, trying to work up enthusiasm for dinner, when Talon strolled through the back door.

Immediately she glanced toward the granite countertops for something to throw at his head.

The ceramic cookie jar would make a satisfying projectile, but it probably wouldn't cause much damage. While the knives stuck in a wooden block would draw blood, but only if he couldn't dodge them.

Highly unlikely.

She was debating between the coffeemaker and the blender when he prowled forward to toss a white paper bag on the polished oak table that matched the china cabinet filled with family heirlooms.

"Here."

She glared at him, hating the fact that her body was already reacting to his presence.

Not just the easing of her nausea that had become progressively worse during his absence, but the immediate awareness that shivered through her.

God. How could her nipples be hardening beneath her sweatshirt and her pussy already be dampening in preparation for his hard, uncompromising entry?

Okay, he was gorgeous.

A tall, stunningly handsome warrior with a lean, sculpted body and eyes that appeared more jade than gold in fading light.

She was mad as hell at him, but her body craved him as if…as if he'd used one of her love potions on her.

In a desperate effort to ease the destructive tide of lust that was as unwanted as it was unexpected, Isi pointed toward the white bag.

"What is it?"

He leaned forward, pulling out the plastic bowl and removing the lid. "Gumbo."

Isi's eyes widened as the mouthwatering smell teased at her nose. There was only one place that made gumbo that smelled like heaven.

"That's my…" She cut off her words, unwilling to reveal any part of herself to the ruthless Hunter.

"Favorite?" he murmured, moving to the cabinets to open a door and extract a spoon. Returning to the table, he put the spoon in the bowl of gumbo before glancing at her rigid form with an unreadable expression. "I know."

Her frown deepened.

She knew the Pantera could screw with humans' minds, but she'd never heard that they could read people's thoughts.

"How?"

His lips twisted. "I was just leaving your shop when a female stormed up to me demanding to know where you were and why she hadn't heard from you."

"Emile." The older woman owned the restaurant across the street from her shop, and not only made the best gumbo in all of Louisiana, but she watched over Isi like a mother hen. Isi's heart clenched with sudden fear. "What did you do to her?"

"I told her that you had been ill and that I was taking care of you." He pointed toward the bowl. "She insisted that her gumbo was necessary to your healing."

Isi shook her head in disbelief.

Even dressed in a pair of faded jeans and well-worn LSU T-shirt Talon looked like a dangerous, potentially deadly predator.

"She believed you?"

"Why wouldn't she? It's the truth." He pulled out a chair. "Eat."

She sucked in a deep breath, savoring the scent of seafood and rice in rich broth. It smelled incredible, but her stomach rebelled at the mere thought of indulging in such a spicy meal.

"I don't think I can."

His lips flattened. "Don't be stubborn. I can sense your hunger."

She folded her arms over her rumbling stomach, hoping that it was the physical hunger he sensed and not the heat that had nothing to do with the steamy bayou night.

"I can't keep it down," she muttered.

"Ah." Comprehension flared in the golden jade eyes. Then, astonishingly, he held out his arms. "Come here."

She took an awkward step backward. "No way."

"Stubborn," he breathed, moving around the table and prowling toward her.

Her ass hit the edge of the counter, halting her retreat.

"What the hell are you doing?" she rasped as he continued forward, not stopping until he was pressed tight against her.

He wrapped his arms around her, lowering his head until she was surrounded in the heat and musk of him.

"Making you better," he murmured.

"Don't…" She forgot what she was going to say as the nausea eked away, replaced by a warm sense of pleasure. Even the throbbing pain at the base of her skull disappeared. "Oh, dammit," she growled, dropping her head against his chest. She knew she should be fighting. The man had called her evil, for christ's sake. Asshole. But it felt so damned good.

Sucking in a deep breath, she concentrated on the delectable musk that seeped deep inside her, chasing away the last of her sickness.

Not that she wasn't acutely aware of his hand that rubbed up and down her back with a shockingly tender motion. Or his warm breath that brushed her cheek. Or even the hardening thrust of his arousal that pressed into her lower stomach.

But for now, it was the glorious sensation of well-being that made her sigh in pleasure.

"Can you eat now?" he asked.

"Yes."

Without warning, Talon scooped her off her feet and carried her toward the table. Then, instead of putting her down, he sat on a wooden chair and tucked her in his lap.

"Talon—"

"Shh." He reached for the bowl of gumbo, placing it directly in front of her. "Eat."

Once again she knew she should fight.

This new and improved Talon was obviously some trick.

She didn't believe for a second that he actually gave a shit if she were suffering.

But it'd been weeks since she'd actually had an appetite and the gumbo smelled so damned good.

Why not enjoy her dinner?

She had plenty of time to be pissed at him after she ate.

Grabbing the spoon, she scooped out a massive bite of the gumbo, shoving it into her mouth with an unashamed lack of female manners.

She groaned as the taste of crawfish and exotic spices hit her tongue. "Oh, god." She hurriedly scooped more of the gumbo into her mouth. "It's heaven."

Talon remained silent as she worked her way through her meal, his hand continuing its soothing path up and down her back and his gaze locked on her face. Isi did her best to ignore him. Well, as much as any female could ignore a six foot two puma shifter with the face of a fallen angel and a blatant sensuality that rubbed against her skin like plush velvet.

Eating the last bite, Isi managed not to lick the bowl—barely—and dropped the spoon onto the table. Then she heaved a deep sigh of satisfaction, savoring the sensation of being full.

"I could put that look on your face," Talon's dark voice whispered in her ear, one hand cupping the back of her neck while the other grasped her hip, pressing her against his thick cock. "In fact, I already did."

She narrowed her gaze. So now they were going from pretending he was some sort of nurturing saint to the smooth seduction routine?

"You're so full of shit," she muttered.

He nibbled a path down the line of her jaw, his hips lifting so he could rub his erection against the soft flesh of her ass.

"But you want me."

She shivered, need thundering through her body. Yes, she wanted him. Dammit. It was taking every ounce of her self-control not to turn so she was straddling him, pressing herself against the length of his cock to ease her ruthless need.

But she'd spent the entire day convincing herself that she wasn't going to give *Talon the Bastard* another chance to humiliate her.

He'd called her evil.

He believed she was fated to destroy his people.

She'd had enough people in her life judging her without ever knowing a thing about her, thank you very fucking much.

"Why were you in my store?" she demanded, needing to remind herself she couldn't trust this Pantera any farther than she could toss him.

He gave a low growl, his fingers tightening on her neck before he blew out a frustrated sigh and reached into his pocket to pull out his cellphone.

With a flick of his finger, he brought up his photos, choosing one that was clearly taken in front of her shop.

"This," he said.

She frowned in confusion. "My van?"

His finger touched the emblem painted on the back panel. A raven flying across a full moon.

"This is the symbol of Shakpi," he murmured. "Our enemy."

She stiffened in his arms. Even expecting the blunt accusation, she flinched.

"I didn't paint the van," she muttered before she could halt the words.

"I know," he said with surprising certainty, tossing his phone on the table. "Your employee Derek designed it."

She sent him a startled glance. How the hell did he know about Derek?

"Yes. He said it would bring in more customers. I just liked it because—" She lifted her hand toward her birthmark only to drop it as she recalled his assurance that the blemish was a physical manifestation of her evilness. She shrugged. "I thought it was cool."

He held her gaze, his hand moving to lightly trace the dark spot on her collarbone. "Because of this."

His touch blazed through her like a wildfire, scorching her nerves until they were unbearably sensitive.

Which only pissed her off.

She didn't want Talon to be the one man who could make her crave his touch. To make her so hungry she could barely think.

At least…she *shouldn't* want it to be him.

"So you went to my shop looking for my tails and horns and pitchfork," she muttered, her nipples hardening in anticipation of his touch. "Did you find them?"

"I found Derek," he admitted, leaning forward to replace his fingers with the destructive touch of his lips. "And he confessed you weren't involved with the traitors."

She shuddered, her gaze locked on the savage beauty of his face as he used his tongue to trace the distinctive birthmark.

"And yet you don't trust me," she husked, barely able to breathe.

His fingers slipped into the short strands of her hair, tugging back her head so his lips could explore the satin length of her neck.

"I don't trust my judgment when you're near."

She tried to squelch the moan that was wrenched from her throat. "What the hell is that supposed to mean?"

"The prophecy says you're destined to destroy me." His fingers skimmed from her hip to tease the bare skin of her lower back. Then, as his teeth nipped the sensitive spot where her neck met her shoulder, he moved his hand to discover the ribbon that laced together the back of her tiny top. With one tug her silky fabric was falling down to expose her bare breasts. Talon hissed as he pulled back to admire his handiwork, the jade that rimmed his eyes darkening with a brutal hunger. "But when I look at you all I see is how desperately I want you."

"Talon," she breathed, unable to disguise the edge of yearning that thickened her voice.

His fingers tightened in her hair. Possessive. Demanding.

"Say it again." It was an order, not a request.

"Talon."

Isi was lost in the unyielding heat of his eyes, feeling as if she were slowly melting beneath the potent heat of his desire.

What the hell was wrong with her?

She better than anyone understood the need to protect herself from the monsters that filled her world. The pervs, the pimps and the users who were constant threats to young girls on their own.

So why now, when she was trapped in the Wildlands and surrounded by her enemies, was she so eager to make herself utterly vulnerable? She should be kicking some serious feline butt, not battling the urge to sink her hands in that thick, golden hair and kiss him senseless.

Of course, maybe she was looking at this from the wrong angle, she told herself as he dipped his head so he could use the very tip of his tongue to tease at her nipple.

Christ. Why not accept that she wanted this man, for whatever reason, and use him, just as he was no doubt using her?

If he intended to hold her prisoner, she might as well get a mind-blowing orgasm out of the deal, shouldn't she?

Not giving herself time to consider the numerous faults in her clouded logic, Isi reached down to yank her top off the rest of the way, before grabbing his T-shirt and performing the same service.

She trembled at the sight of his smooth, bronzed skin that was stretched tautly over the hard, chiseled muscles. His chest was broad and tapered to a flat stomach with a six-pack her fingers lingered to explore. He was sleek and well-toned without unnecessary bulk. And his hands...lord, they were magic as they cupped her breasts with a possessive touch that sent streaks of heat directly to all her most intimate places.

He was hard, male perfection top to bottom, and every place in between.

The bastard.

"This means nothing," she muttered.

"Tell yourself whatever you want, darling." A slow, wicked smile curved his lips. "But don't doubt for a second that I intend to give you a night you're never going to forget."

"Arrogant."

He nipped the tip of her nipple, making Isi's heart stutter in shock. How could the tiny pain send jolts of ecstasy through her?

"Confident in my ability to please you."

"You're so full of shit…" Her taunting words were completely ruined as his lips closed around the nipple, sucking her with an expertise that had her trembling with need. "Oh."

"Oh, indeed," he growled, moving his lips to her collarbone. "I fucking want to taste you all over."

His enticing musk invaded her senses, embedding itself so deep inside her that she feared it would remain a permanent part of her.

"What are you doing to me?" she muttered, her hands running a restless path down his chest.

His soft laugh brushed over her cheek as he reached down to grasp the button on her jeans, helping her wriggle out of them before tossing them across the room.

"Nothing you aren't doing to me," he muttered, arching back to run a searing gaze over her body now covered in nothing more than a red thong.

Isi shivered, the gold and jade gaze a near tangible force as it moved from the tattoo that ran the length of her neck to linger on her breasts that felt oddly heavy.

"Why does your musk make me feel better?"

His hands glided down to grip her hips, his lips tracing the curve of her breast.

"Actually, I don't have a clue."

"Can you use it as a—"

His hands gripped her hips, abruptly lifting her up so he could tug her to face him, settling her back down so she straddled his lap. A groan was wrenched from her throat as the hard line of his cock hit her tender clitoris, nearly making her come.

"A what?"

She struggled to think as he returned his attention to her aching breasts. "An aphrodisiac?"

"It can be." He tilted back his head to flash her a grin filled with wicked promise. "But trust me, I don't need an aphrodisiac to make you hot and bothered."

She dug her nails into the smooth skin of his shoulders. "Don't mock me."

He continued to tease her nipple, rubbing his cock with flawless precision against her. Oh...shit. It felt good. Violently, insanely good.

"Mocking is not what I want to be doing with you," he said, kissing a path between her breasts.

"Talon."

With a low groan, Talon lifted his head to claim her lips in a kiss that demanded complete surrender. Hunger blasted through her, searing away any hope of resistance.

"Before this night is over I intend to hear you scream my name," he husked against her lips. "Over and over."

She pressed against his erection in blatant invitation. "You talk a big game, but how do I know you can deliver?"

He chuckled, blazing a path of kisses down her throat. "Don't ever challenge a Pantera, darling. I might not ever allow you out of my bed again."

She instinctively shied from his possessive tone.

"I'll leave your bed whenever I want to," she warned, deliberately rubbing against his cock. She smiled at his violent shudder of pleasure. "And if you think you can manipulate me with sex, you'd better think again."

"Isi," he growled, his eyes narrowing. "Can you stop searching for an insult in everything I say?"

"I just don't want you assuming—"

His hands moved over her body, his mouth planting restless kisses between her breasts and down the quivering plane of her stomach.

"There's no assumption," he rasped. "Just you and me. Let yourself go."

Isi gasped when he grabbed her by the waist and before she knew what was happening, she found herself perched on the edge of the table with Talon kneeling between her spread legs. Leaning forward, he dipped his tongue into her belly button, a shocking bolt of pleasure aiming straight between her legs.

Holy shit. Talon truly was a Hunter.

He went straight for the kill.

She planted her hands on the table behind her, feeling as if she was being assaulted with sensations. The bold exploration of his hands, the moist caress of his tongue, the heady musk that stirred her senses.

It was like being tossed into the middle of a raging vortex.

"Just for tonight," she managed to rasp.

He lifted his head to stare at her with open amusement. "You won't budge an inch, will you, Isi?"

"Never." Way past the point of no return, Isi decided the only thing left was to give in to the inevitable. Running her hands up the curve of his neck, she plunged her fingers into his hair. "Now shut up and prove you're more than just talk."

***

Hell no, she didn't just go there.

What Pantera could resist a blatant challenge to his manhood?

Especially if proving his manhood meant taking this female over and over, until she was too sated with pleasure to move.

Of course, he would prefer if she wasn't watching him with that wary defiance, as if convinced he was plotting some nefarious means to hurt her. Not that he could blame her. He'd given her little reason to trust him.

Something that was going to change.

Gently spreading her legs wider, Talon allowed his hands to skim up her bare thighs, his gaze drinking in the sight of the tiny scrap of lace that was all that hid her delectable pussy.

His heart thundered as his fingers headed toward the sweet spot, feeling off-balanced by the intensity of his desire.

He expected the male part of him to be ready and eager to have sex with this female. Even when he was trying to convince himself she couldn't be trusted, he was battling his ruthless desire. But the hunger of his cat was unexpected.

He'd never had his animal so close to the surface during sex. It was intensely erotic to have his pleasure echoed within the cat.

He didn't question why his animal would be so intensely fascinated by Isi.

Not when he was already beginning to suspect the truth.

She hissed out a sharp breath as the power of his cat glowed in his eyes, filling the room with a golden light. Not that she was afraid. Not his foolishly brave Isi.

It was the same raw hunger that clawed at him.

"I need to taste you," he said thickly, his fingers at last reaching the edge of her thong. "I can't wait any longer."

Her eyes darkened, her hands tightening in his hair as he allowed a claw to form, slicing through the delicate fabric. His cat growled in pleasure as the satin fluttered to the table, leaving her bare to his avid gaze.

Damn.

She was beautiful.

His mouth watered as he slowly leaned forward, closely monitoring her reaction. As desperately as he wanted her, he was prepared to halt the second she revealed any hesitation.

She watched him from beneath lowered lashes, her face flushed with passion. Then, for one breathless second she tensed, her expression troubled. Talon swallowed a curse.

Isi had been forced to the Wildlands, and then bullied into staying.

He wasn't going to pressure her into sex if she had doubts.

But before he could pull away, she tightened her fingers in his hair and tugged him forward.

He met her smoldering gaze. "You're sure?"

"I'm sure." She gave a slow nod, her dark hair with its blue highlights shimmering like satin in the dim light. "Don't you dare stop."

He studied her for a long moment, waiting until he could see the frantic urgency smoldering in her midnight eyes.

Only then did he lean forward, at last allowing his tongue to stroke through her slick fold.

His eyes slid shut in pleasure.

Christ.

She tasted of magnolia and woman. Sweet, luscious cream and power.

Talon's cock twitched, pressing painfully against the zipper of his jeans.

He needed to be in her.

He needed to mark her. Not only with his passion, but with his musk. Hell, with his very essence.

The thought should have been terrifying. Instead, nothing had ever felt more right.

This female was precisely what he needed. Strong. Independent. But with a heart that was aching for the opportunity to love.

They'd both lost their families and deep inside they were both searching for a place to call home.

Something they could build together.

Isi, however, instinctively shied from his possessive animal instinct.

"Keep your cat leashed, fur ball," she muttered.

His hands grabbed the curve of her waist, holding her still as his tongue found her swollen clitoris.

"My cat is the least of your concerns, darling."

"You...oh, shit."

For once, she was speechless as Talon flicked his tongue over her tender nub, her hips rocking upward in a silent plea for release. Again and again he stroked through her damp heat, his cat snarling in satisfaction as he wrenched a low whimper from the stubborn female.

In this moment nothing was as important as giving her more pleasure than she'd ever experienced before.

"Isi, come for me," he commanded in thick tones.

She moaned, her body trembling as she hovered on the edge of climax. "No, Talon," she breathed. "I want you inside me."

Her soft plea sliced through him, and he reluctantly pulled back. As much as he wanted to taste her orgasm on his tongue, he wanted to please her more.

And if that meant waiting to give her an orgasm when he was buried deep inside her...then that's exactly what he would do.

Gritting his teeth, Talon rose to his feet, hastily yanking off his boots so he could dispose of his jeans. The taste of Isi lingered on his tongue, the scent of magnolias making his head spin.

Unaware of how close he was to the edge, or perhaps simply enjoying her power over him, Isi stared at the throbbing length of his cock, a hectic passion glowing in her dark eyes.

He reached to grasp her around the waist, hauling her up his body to claim her lips with an intensity that branded her as his.

"I can't wait," he muttered.

She deliberately wrapped her long legs around his hips, her smile smug. "I thought cats were known for their stamina."

"Hold on, darling." Talon lowered onto the chair, the tip of his cock at the entrance to her body. Then, with a slow, ruthless thrust he pushed himself into her damp channel, not halting until his balls were pressed tight against her ass.

"Oh, god...yes," she husked.

Running his hands up her back, Talon sucked the tip of her breast between his lips, relishing her low moan of pleasure. She fit as tight as a glove around him, making him tremble with the effort to wait until she was accustomed to his penetration.

"You feel perfect," he rasped. "Ride me, Isi."

Planting her hands on his shoulders, she lifted her hips, drawing him out to the very tip before slowly sinking back down, burying him deep inside her. Talon muttered a curse, his hands gripping her hips as he battled against the climax that was already building.

Dammit. She'd just challenged his stamina. There was no way in hell he was going to come before he was certain she was satisfied.

But never before had sex called to both the man and cat inside him.

Sweat gathered on his brow as he concentrated on the mesmerizing beauty of her midnight eyes. The wary suspicion was gone, the pupils dilated as she quickened her pace.

His hips lifted to meet her downward strokes, his growl of satisfaction filling the air as she leaned down to sink her teeth into the flesh at the base of his neck, drawing blood.

The air was saturated with the perfume of her arousal, her slender body bowing above him as she tipped back her head and lost herself in the pleasure.

"Talon," she cried softly, a desperate edge in her voice as her orgasm neared.

"Darling," he whispered. "Trust me."

"I…" She moaned in pleasure as Talon tightened his grip on her hips, driving deep into her with an unyielding tempo. "Yes, that's it."

"I have you, Isi," he swore, his hand cupping the back of her head and tugging her down so he could kiss her with savage pleasure. "And I'm never letting go."

Their tongues tangled, their bodies moving together at a frantic pace. Then, just when Talon feared he was going to explode, he felt Isi stiffen, her cry of completion muffled against his lips.

Talon felt his claws emerge, slicing through the lower skin of her back as her climax clutched at his cock, his hips slamming upward as he unleashed his passion in a flurry of wild hunger.

His cat howled in satisfaction as his orgasm burst through him, the violent jolts of pleasure radiating through his entire body.

Realization hit him at the same moment.

This woman was his.

His mate.

His destiny.

For all eternity.

CHAPTER FIVE

Talon managed to stagger up the stairs with a limp Isi in his arms, his knees still weak from the intense pleasure that had exploded through his body.

A part of him had wanted to linger in the kitchen. To lay her across the table and eat his dinner off the satin magnolia of her skin before sliding his aching cock back into her body and stroking them both to paradise.

But a more logical part of him understood they needed to talk before he indulged his ravenous hunger.

Not the least of which, he had to somehow explain that in the heat of their passion he'd marked her as his mate.

Yeah. That was going to go over well.

He grimaced, hoping she didn't slice off his balls in his sleep.

Oddly, he didn't question how he'd gone from considering her the enemy to accepting her as his mate with such ease.

His cat had known she belonged to him the second it'd caught her scent. It just took the male side of him a bit longer to figure it out.

Now both were in agreement.

Isi was his mate.

And somehow he had to convince her to accept him.

A task he'd made a hell of a lot more difficult when he'd accused her of being an enemy to the Pantera.

Entering his bedroom, Talon crossed to the wide bed and gently placed her in the middle of the mattress, crawling to lie beside her. Gently he pulled her into his arms, her weary head snuggled on his shoulder.

It felt...right.

Not only having Isi in his arms, but being in this cottage that had been empty for so many years.

It was almost as if he could sense his parents' approval.

Heaving a soft sigh, Isi tilted back her head, her exotic beauty shrouded in shadows.

"That shouldn't have happened," she muttered.

He smiled wryly. Those were the words he'd been waiting to hear since she'd collapsed in utter completion.

"Why?"

She struggled to reconstruct the brittle barriers that she kept between herself and the world.

"Obviously because I don't have sex with people who think I'm evil."

He slid a finger beneath her chin, easily becoming lost in the dark beauty of her eyes. "I don't think you're evil."

A hint of vulnerability touched her pale face. "Then what do you think?"

His thumb brushed her lower lip, his gaze lightly moving over the fragile features to the diamond piercings that shimmered on her nose. They only added to her unique beauty. As did her tattoos and even her birthmark.

They were the proof that this woman was as much a warrior as he was.

"I think that you were given a shitty start to life, but you've not only managed to survive, but to become an intelligent, competent woman able to create her own business," he murmured in soft tones. "And one who is courageous and loyal enough to be willing to suffer just to help a sister who was a complete stranger to you."

Her expression remained stubbornly defiant. "Nice, but we both know I'm staying because the elders want me dead."

He leaned down to snatch a brief, utterly carnal kiss. "Lie to yourself if you want, but you can't lie to me," he murmured. Over the past hours he'd started to understand the gentle female beneath the hard façade. "If it weren't for Ashe you would have disappeared the night you were brought to the Wildlands."

She sucked in a sharp breath. "Don't say that."

He frowned, easily sensing her distress. "Why are you so scared to admit your feelings?"

"Because feelings are for suckers."

He arched a brow. "Suckers?"

"They're anchors that weigh you down," she said, a sudden tension humming through her slender body. "To survive you have to keep moving."

Talon's heart squeezed, easily able to picture Isi as a little girl, lost and terrified in an institutional setting that taught her emotions were a weakness.

"Or you can depend on those who love you to keep you safe," he assured her, his hand running down her bare back to linger on the healing scratches that were proof of their mating.

She shivered, reacting to the tenderness of the mark. "I don't depend on anyone but myself."

"You can depend on me."

She pressed her hands to his chest. "No."

"Yes." He held her gaze, his expression fierce. "You feel it, Isi. Don't deny it."

The truth flared through her eyes...the knowledge that they were fated to be together.

Not that she was going to accept her destiny.

Not without a fight.

"And what about the elders?" she demanded, doing her best to throw fences up between them. "They believe I'm destined to destroy you."

He clenched his jaw. He didn't have an answer.

Not yet.

But he was damned certain that she wasn't any harbinger of doom.

The problem was how to prove it.

"How did you learn about the Pantera?" he abruptly demanded.

She shrugged. "Everyone's heard the rumors of the savage half-men half-beasts that live in the swamps."

"Most assume we're a myth," he pointed out. "But you specifically cater to my people."

The rigid tension began to ease from her muscles, her fingers drawing absent patterns on his chest. Talon trembled beneath her soft caress, his cat purring in contentment.

Christ, he would walk through fire just for her touch.

"I was always fascinated with mixing my tattoo inks with different materials," she murmured, seemingly unaware she'd completely domesticated him. "And the voodoo priestess who helped train me in creating my spells and potions encouraged me to use malachite. She was the one who introduced me to my first Pantera. Others followed."

Talon latched onto the obvious connection. "Was the voodoo priestess called Lady Cerise?"

"No." She stared at him, genuine fear flashing through her eyes. "How do you know that name?"

His hand lifted to cup her nape, gently rubbing his thumb along the side of her neck. "Your friend Derek was approached by her," he said. "That's how he ended up in your shop."

Her breath tangled in her throat, her eyes wide. "Shit."

Concern clenched his heart. Isi clearly felt threatened by the woman.

"Who is she?"

Isi shivered. "She first approached me in Baton Rouge. I was already a student of Esme, but Lady Cerise continued to come into the voodoo shop where I was working, claiming that she could teach me magic that would be far more powerful than my potions."

"You weren't interested?"

"There was something…evil about her." She narrowed her gaze, determinedly remembering his stupid reaction to her birthmark. "Truly evil."

With a deliberate motion he dipped his head down to stroke his lips over the dark mark on her collarbone, silently apologizing for having hurt her.

"So you declined her offer?" he murmured, his lips brushing her skin.

She heaved a rueful sigh, accepting that he wasn't going to let her keep him at a distance. Instead, she threaded her fingers through his hair as his lips moved to the fascinating spot where her shoulder met her neck.

"More than that," she said, her tone growing distracted. "I fled Baton Rouge when she took an apartment in the same building where I was living, and moved to New Orleans. She was seriously creeping me out."

"She followed you?" Talon demanded, grabbing her hand and lowering it toward the aching length of his cock.

Without further urging she wrapped her fingers around his hard length, stroking down to his heavy sack.

A smug smile touched her lips at his tortured groan.

"Yes, but she kept her distance so I did my best to ignore her."

"There must be something that she wants from you," Talon said, trying to put together the pieces of the dangerous puzzle.

He now knew that the enemy had been keeping track of Isi, and that they were searching for someone who was obviously important to their cause. He'd also made certain that the Suits had eyes on Derek who would eventually lead them to the warehouse where Lon and his crew were hopefully hidden.

Later he would send someone to New Orleans to search for the mysterious Lady Cerise.

Those were all steps in the right direction.

For now, he intended to concentrate on his new mate.

Her fingers began to pump up and down his erection with a steady pace, and he made a raw sound of approval.

"Lady Cerise isn't the only one to want something from me," she muttered.

With a strangled groan, Talon rolled so he was perched on top of her slender body, framing her face in his hands.

"All I want is your happiness," he swore, holding her wary gaze so she couldn't mistake his sincerity. "And I promise, no matter what it takes, that's what I'll give you."

Her lips parted, her expression a mix between wariness and a grudging hope.

"Talon."

"You know you're mine. You feel it here." He lowered his head to press his lips directly over her thundering heart. "And here." He moved to lick the tip of one tightly clenched nipple before spreading his kisses down the flat plane of her stomach. "And here."

"Oh god," she moaned, her legs instinctively spreading as he licked through the warm, delectable sweetness.

"And most definitely here," he rasped, thrusting his tongue deep into her body. She gasped, her body arching as she clenched the sheet beneath her. "Admit it, Isi," he urged, continuing to torment her as she remained stubbornly silent. "Tell me that you belong to me."

"I…" Her words broke off in a blissful sigh, her hands reaching to grasp his hair as he expertly tongued her to a swift climax. "Yes."

"Yes, what?"

"I belong to you."

He lifted his head, meeting her dazed eyes. "Forever."

***

Isi understood on a basic level that she'd lost her mind.

There could be no other explanation for the joy that bubbled through her as she lay entangled on the bed with her annoying cat.

Hers.

Talon was right.

She'd felt a connection to him before they'd ever met.

The scent of his musk had not only eased her illness, but it'd stirred a longing deep inside her that she hadn't fully appreciated until Talon had appeared.

It was as if her heart and soul had already realized that she'd found the man destined to break through her barriers to claim the lonely woman beneath.

Just the sort of corny, fairy-tale ending that used to make her gag.

As far as she was concerned, Disney was selling a load of crap to young girls.

And then Talon had crashed into her life.

The prickly, impossibly arrogant cat had done his best to piss her off from their first meeting.

So was it any wonder she was struggling to admit to her growing bond?

Not that Talon was going to allow her the time or space to come to terms with their intense, rapidly changing relationship.

He was leaning on his elbow, glaring down at her with a narrowed gaze.

"You said it," he accused. "You agreed you belonged to me."

She tried to be annoyed by his insistence. Unfortunately, she could barely form a coherent thought as she studied the spectacular beauty of his face. Christ. No man should have such stunning eyes. It was completely unfair.

"You can't hold a person responsible for anything they say in bed." She said, her voice pathetically weak. "That's the rule."

"Whose rule?" he demanded.

"Mine."

He leaned down until they were nose to nose, the light picking up the copper highlights in his hair.

"This is my bed and my rules. You said you belong to me, so you do."

She shook her head. She might have shoved him away if her body hadn't been too lethargic from her last explosive orgasm.

"You can't just make the decision."

Talon abruptly stiffened. Almost as if her words had struck a nerve.

"Actually, I should probably admit that…"

Isi arched a brow as he hesitated. Since when did arrogant, "I'm always right" Talon pause to consider his words?

"What?" she prompted.

"That I marked you."

She stared at him, waiting to hear the punch line. Surely he couldn't actually be saying what she thought he was saying.

"You mean…you *marked me*, marked me?" she demanded. "As in mating mark?"

His expression was somber as he ensnared her gaze, forcing her to accept that this was no joke.

"Yes."

She licked her dry lips. "What does that mean?"

"You know what it means." His hand slid down her spine, lingering at the sensitive spot on her lower back where he'd marked her. "You're mine."

Isi struggled to be pissed at his outrageous proclamation.

What right did he have to mark her?

She wasn't a piece of property he could just claim.

She was a thoroughly independent woman who had no intention of tying herself to another human being, let alone a Pantera.

But she wasn't pissed.

In fact, she had a disturbing suspicion that if she'd just let down her guard she would discover that his mark was the inevitable conclusion to their heated mating dance.

"Don't you think you should have asked me if I wanted to be yours?" she forced herself to demand.

His eyes were more jade than gold as he studied her face with a tenderness that made her heart pound in her chest.

"It's not a question of choice." His fingers lightly feathered over his marks of possession, the caress sending erotic jolts of pleasure through her. "At least not for me."

A surge of satisfaction burst through her before she could tilt her chin to a defiant angle. "And me?"

He held her gaze, his musk teasing at her senses like the finest aphrodisiac. "I would never hold you against your will, Isi," he swore. "Whether you decide to accept the mating is in your hands."

"And if I don't?" she challenged. "What happens to you?"

A raw, starkly painful emotion darkened his eyes. "I will continue to try and earn your love for the rest of my life."

Isi bit her bottom lip.

It was, of course, the absolutely perfect thing to say.

The bastard.

"Oh," she whispered.

His head dipped down to kiss her. Then he gave a sudden hiss, jumping off the bed and rushing to the window. "Shit."

Alarm blasted through Isi as she shoved herself off the bed. "What?

"Put this on," he commanded, tossing her one of his T-shirts before reaching to pull on a pair of faded jeans.

Isi didn't argue, tugging the T-shirt over her head. It fell to mid-thigh, covering the basics.

Not that she really gave a shit what she was or wasn't exposing. It was obvious something bad was happening.

"Talon, what is it?" she rasped.

His face was grim. "Intruders."

Oh, hell. Her heart squeezed with fear.

"Human?"

"No." He headed toward the door of the bedroom.

"Where are you going?"

"To get rid of the trespassers."

Panic thundered through her as she chased after him, down the stairs and into the kitchen. She didn't have to ask who was out there. Talon wouldn't be so on edge if it was anyone but the elders.

"Not alone," she pleaded. "We have to call Raphael."

Never slowing his determined stride, Talon snatched his cellphone off the table and tossed it in her direction.

"You call," he said, sending her a warning glare. "And don't come out of this house."

"But…" She muttered a curse as Talon stepped out of the cottage, firmly closing the door behind him. "Dammit."

With shaky hands she pressed on the phone and scrolled to find Raphael's number. Within seconds she heard a familiar voice.

"What?"

"It's Isi," she said, her voice a raspy croak. "Come to the cottage. And hurry."

She placed the phone on the counter and headed to pull open the door.

Talon could toss out as many orders as he wanted, but she'd be damned if she was going to allow him to fight her battles.

She stepped onto the porch, her gaze moving to the two large, male Pantera in human form who bracketed a strange mist just inside the front gate. She felt a terrifying chill spear through her heart as the mist parted to reveal three female puma.

The three ranged in shades from brown to a pristine white, with different colored eyes. But they all shared the same aura of ancient power.

The sort of power she couldn't hope to battle.

The elders.

She gave a startled jump as they suddenly spoke. Not just because they combined their voices to speak as one, but because they didn't speak aloud. Instead she heard them in her mind.

"Step aside, Talon," they commanded of the man who blocked the pathway to the house.

The stubborn cat folded his arms over his chest. "No."

The mist trembled around the elders, as if astonished by Talon's refusal to obey. Odd. Isi had known him only a few days and she could have informed them that he had an allergy to being told what to do.

"The female must be sacrificed if we are to rescue our lands from destruction," they said in unison.

Isi wrapped her arms around her waist, glaring at the pumas. Bitches.

Talon growled low in his throat. "You don't know that her sacrifice will do anything to save the Wildlands."

"It was foretold."

"Prophecies can be interpreted to mean anything," Talon argued.

The elders regarded him with flat gazes, a sudden heat prickling in the air.

"Will you risk the future of your people to protect the female?"

His answer came without hesitation. "Yes."

Isi forgot to breathe, her gaze locked on Talon's broad back as he stood between her and the powerful females who wanted her dead.

Never had anyone stood up for her. Let alone risked their life to protect her.

God...Talon was willing to sacrifice his people.

The last layer of her protective barriers shattered as the bond between them settled into place, irrevocably binding them together.

There was the sensation of surprise before the voices of the elders echoed through her brain.

"You've mated her."

"Fate mated us," Talon countered.

Mated. Yes. The word was perfect for the bond she felt for Talon.

But even as she adjusted to the knowledge that her future was forever bound to the cat, a fierce fury was racing through her.

She'd been alone for as long as she could remember, and now, just when she had the opportunity to share her world with a man who she loved and a sister who needed her, the damned elders were threatening to snatch it all away.

"It changes nothing," they were saying, their gazes studying her with a grim determination.

"Fuck that," Talon snarled. "It changes everything."

"You will give us the female or you will die," the elders warned.

Talon shrugged. "Then I die."

"No."

The horrified denial was jerked from Isi's lips as she rushed down the steps to stand beside her mate.

Talon turned to glare at her with a smoldering frustration. "I told you to stay in the house."

She lifted a hand to brush her fingers through his silky hair, her heart twisting with a fear that had nothing to do with her own danger, and everything to do with this man who'd somehow become a vital part of her existence.

"I won't let them hurt you."

His expression tightened with a savage need to protect her. "Not your choice."

"Yes," she said softly. "It is."

"Dammit, Isi," he growled. "You're not alone anymore. We're in this together."

Together. A wistful smile touched her lips.

It was ironic. She spent her whole life avoiding relationships, certain they would demand a price she wasn't willing to pay. Now, when she was facing certain death, she realized that there was no price to love.

It didn't take.

It gave.

Everything.

"Not if it means watching you die," she said in husky tones. "Anything but that."

His cat glowed in his eyes, his emotions scalding the air with heat as the two male Pantera rapidly approached.

"Isi…no."

Her finger brushed his lips before she was turning to haul ass toward the side gate, glancing over her shoulder as she flipped off the elders.

"You want me? Then catch me, you bitches."

CHAPTER SIX

Talon was braced for the two Hunters who charged toward him, prepared to kill them if that's what it took to protect his mate.

It didn't matter that he'd trained with them. Or that they were only following the commands of the elders.

If they stood between him and the woman who was his other half then they had to die.

On the point of shifting, Talon was caught off-guard when the nearest Pantera halted, pointing a small crossbow in his direction.

What the hell?

He dodged to the side as the small bolt whizzed toward him, striking him in the upper thigh.

The weapon wasn't large enough to cause permanent damage, but Talon swiftly realized that he was in trouble.

Already a thick potion laced with malachite was pumping through his bloodstream, caging his cat and weakening him.

God. Dammit.

"Don't interfere, Talon," the voices of the elders thundered through his mind as they went in pursuit of

Isi who'd already vaulted over the gate and disappeared into the marshes.

The two guards followed behind them, leaving Talon to collapse against the stairs of the porch.

Black fury engulfed him, his cat roaring in distress as the scent of his mate faded.

On hands and knees he tried to claw his way toward the gate, refusing to give up despite the knowledge that he'd never get to Isi before she was caught by the elders.

He would fucking drag himself across the entire country to get to his mate.

He'd managed to crawl halfway down the path when he heard a startled curse and Raphael was abruptly kneeling beside him.

"What the hell is going on?"

Talon reached out to grab Raphael's hand. "The elders...they have Isi. You have to save her."

"Shit," Raphael muttered. "What did they do to you?"

Talon struggled to lift his head, meeting Raphael's eyes that glowed with a luminous rage.

"Malachite," he managed to mutter.

With another round of foul curses, Raphael ran his hand over Talon's trembling body, at last locating the dart.

"This is going to hurt," the older cat warned, yanking out the dart before he used his dagger to cut a deep incision and sucking out the potion like it was snake poison.

Instantly Talon began to feel stronger.

With the source of the malachite removed, his natural immune system kicked into gear, beginning to burn away the effects of the mineral.

Forcing himself upright, Talon would have tumbled on his face if Raphael hadn't reached out to wrap an arm around his shoulders, hauling Talon against his side.

"Damn," he growled.

"I've got you," Raphael promised, keeping Talon upright as they headed toward the gate.

Talon's balance remained uncertain and his movements painfully stiff, but he grimly forced himself to keep pace as Raphael led them along the edge of the marsh, the older Pantera's expression intent as he remained locked on the trail.

Then without warning he came to a halt. "Dammit."

Talon clenched his teeth, the need to get to Isi pounding through him with a brutal insistence.

"What?"

Raphael grimaced. "The elders used their mist to mask their scent."

Talon closed his eyes, concentrating on his bond with Isi. "I can find her."

"You're mated?" Raphael demanded in surprise.

"Not now," Talon snarled. "We have to get to Isi."

"Fine. Where are they?"

"The temple."

Raphael gave a sharp nod and together they were headed toward the most sacred section of the Wildlands. Less than fifteen minutes later they approached the wide, cypress bridge that extended across the moonlit bayou.

It was said that the middle of the bridge marked the precise spot where the sisters Opela and Shakpi were born.

And where Opela had sacrificed herself to imprison her evil sister.

Tonight the foot of the bridge was brightly lit with torches. The pools of light surrounded the three elders who sat before Isi who'd been tied to a wooden pier. On each side of her was a male Pantera guard holding a large dagger. Not that they needed the weapons. Isi was not only bound and gagged, but she was barely conscious, with a large bruise already forming on the side of her head where she'd been hit.

Talon roared in outrage, desperately trying to shift so he could rip the bastards to tiny, bloody shreds.

"Stay back." The voices of the elders blasted through his brain, but Talon moved grimly forward.

"Talon." Raphael grabbed his arm, holding him in place. Then he turned to glare at the elders. "Don't do this."

"We have no choice," they replied in unison. "Look at the land. Even here, in this sacred place, the magic is fading."

Talon glanced toward the mossy ground, noticing for the first time that it had turned a sickly shade of brown. A part of him was saddened by the sight of the decay. He was as horrified as any Pantera at the thought that the Wildlands were endangered.

But in this moment, nothing mattered but rescuing Isi.

Raphael spoke directly to the elders. "My baby…the first Pantera in fifty years…will die without her."

The elders never allowed their attention to waver from Isi or the men who both lifted daggers to slice through Isi's forearms, the wounds deep enough to allow blood to drip down her arms and onto the ground.

Talon lunged forward, only to be halted by Raphael. He growled in fury, but the malachite still coursed through his blood, making him too weak to fight the larger Pantera.

"This is the only way to ensure the child will survive," the elders pronounced, hissing in disgust as Isi's blood hit the ground with a loud sizzle, scorching what was left of the dying vegetation. "There. You see. Her blood is toxic."

A shocked silence filled the air as they watched in varying degrees of horror as the blood continued to spread over the ground, leaving blackened earth in its path.

It was as if her blood held a wildfire that destroyed whatever it touched.

Chillingly aware of what was going to happen next, Talon fiercely called on his cat, overcoming the lingering malachite with grim resolution.

In a blur of power he shifted, lunging forward before anyone could react to his abrupt attack.

His roar shook the ground as he rammed into one of the guards who'd dare to hurt Isi, using one brutal swipe of his paw to knock him unconscious. Without hesitation, he was slamming into the second guard, catching him before he could shift and defend himself.

His teeth sank into the man's flesh, but before he could rip out his throat, Raphael was at his side, yelling directly into his ear.

"Wait. Dammit, Talon, look."

Slowly the words penetrated the red haze that filled Talon's mind with the need to kill, forcing him to release his prey and glance where Raphael was pointing.

Astonishment jolted through Talon, jerking him from his cat form to human. Instinctively he moved to stand as a barrier between Isi and the elders, his frantic gaze watching as the blackened earth trembled, as if a powerful force was surging from beneath the ground. Then tiny, tender sprouts of green began to break through the crusty dirt.

"It's starting regrow," he breathed. "She's healing the land."

There was the sensation of furious disbelief as the mist around the elders shimmered in the torchlight.

"It's her death—"

"Stop." Talon took his life in his hands by challenging the powerful females. "You see what's happening." He swept his hand toward the tender green shoots that were beginning to spread. "Are you going to let your stubborn belief that you're always right destroy our hope for the future?"

Raphael moved to stand at his side, his arms folded over his chest. "Talon is right. Until we understand what is happening, we can't risk destroying the female."

There was a long silence, as if the elders were arguing among themselves. Talon swiftly used their distraction to turn back to Isi, using a claw to slice through the ropes that bound her to the pier.

His heart clenched as she tumbled into his arms. She was barely conscious, her body trembling from a combination of pain and shock.

God dammit.

He'd failed her. She was his to protect, but he'd allowed her to be stolen from him and injured.

"Talon." Wrapping her arms around his neck, she buried her face in his throat.

He scooped her off her feet, cradling her against his chest. "I've got you, darling," he swore, his gaze locked on the elders. No one was taking her away. Not ever again. "And I'm never letting you go."

"You have made your point, Talon," the elder with white fur spoke in his head, taking the lead for her sisters. "Although we are not convinced she is harmless, there is enough doubt to delay her death until we have a greater understanding of what is occurring."

"I think I might be able to help." Stepping from the shadows at the edge of the sacred land, a male Pantera offered the elders a low bow. "May I approach?"

The elders spoke in unison. "Welcome, Xavier."

The tall, mocha-toned man with startling blue eyes moved gracefully forward.

Talon felt a leap of hope at the sight of the leader of the Geeks. If anyone had managed to coax the secrets from the computers Talon had brought from Baton Rouge, it would be this brilliant Pantera.

"What did you discover?" he demanded, ignoring the annoyance of the ancient females who clearly felt they should be in charge.

He didn't give shit who he had to piss off.

He was going to do whatever necessary to protect his mate.

Xavier walked forward, his gaze flickering toward the fresh green vegetation on the ground before moving to Isi who remained cradled in Talon's arms.

"I know who our enemies are searching for."

Talon felt a tingle of premonition inch down his spine as Xavier's dark gaze remained locked on Isi.

"Who?" Raphael at last demanded.

"Chayton," the Geek revealed. "Father of Isi and Ashe."

XAVIER

LAURA WRIGHT

CHAPTER ONE

Sweet freedom.

Pool cue in one hand, margarita in the other, Amalie strode across the dusty floor of The Cougar's Den.

Hot damn, she was emancipated.

Granted, it was only for three days and nights, but she planned to make the most out of every second. Clad in her tightest jeans, black high-heeled boots, and a white tank that showed off her young, Hunter's body and plenty of cleavage up top, she felt every male eye move over her as she passed.

Well, every male but one.

Stopping in front of the pool table, she dropped her cue on the playing surface and lifted her glass to her lips. Salty sweet goodness rolled over her tongue and down her throat. She wasn't a big drinker. Shoot, she wasn't a big anything. In fact, this was her first time in The Cougar's Den. For years, she'd heard all about it from the other Hunters. Listened as they regaled her with stories about drunken nights, hard-won pool games, hook-ups with hot males or females. While she went home.

Not tonight, she mused, draining her glass, then eyeing the bartender. Tonight she was cutting loose.

Tonight she was going to know what it felt like to play hard, drink hard and just be a ready and willing single female.

"What do you say, darlin'?"

Mal glanced over her shoulder, spied the male who'd just spoken to her. He was tall, blond and human, and his mouth curved into a wicked smile. "Dance?"

She turned around and faced him. "I didn't know this place had a dance floor."

"They don't," he said. "Not yet anyway."

The male whistled to one of his buddies and the pair grabbed a few tables and pushed them aside.

He turned back to Mal and shrugged. "Nothing fancy, but it'll do. What do you say? I like this song and you're smoking hot."

Mal's heart fluttered in her chest. Sure, she was a kickass Hunter who was capable of bringing down several full-grown males with one hand tied behind her back—part of her training—but in the Wildlands no one ever talked to her like this. Looked at her like this. Like she was desirable and available. It felt so good.

Alcohol snaking through her blood, making her warm and bold, she followed him out onto the makeshift dance floor. The bartender had cranked up the music and a few other couples had already taken advantage of the space.

"Name's Beau," the male said over the music as he started to move.

Mal grinned as she sidled up close to him and started to sway her hips. "Nice to meet you, Beau."

"You too, darlin'." His eyes traveled down her body. "Never seen anything as sexy as you come in here."

"I'm sure that's not true," she said on a husky laugh, her head feeling deliciously fuzzy. "But I appreciate it anyway."

He laughed with her, his dark eyes glittering with interest. They were a handsome set of eyes, deep and soulful, and she could probably get lost in them if it wasn't for the breath-stealing, knee-weakening crystal blue orbs of a certain Pantera male in the room. Eyes she'd been lusting after forever.

Seeing those piercing, highly sexual eyes in her mind, and fueled by inhibition-killing margaritas, she turned her head.

Such a big mistake.

He'd only been in The Cougar's Den for maybe a half hour, but it was enough for him to cause a stir. Not like he could help it. Females just couldn't seem to catch their breath around him, and males were understandably intimated by his size.

Still swaying, Mal ran her hands up the sides of her body as she watched him at the bar. Eating up the metal bar stool he inhabited, Xavier was by far the hottest male specimen that had ever walked the earth. Over six foot four, and all powerful shoulders and broad chest, the gorgeous male looked more like a professional athlete than the head of the Geeks. His skin was the color of wet bark, and his features were sharp and fierce. His dark hair had just been recently cut, buzzed close to his scalp, making his amazing, crystal blue eyes pop. And every time Mal saw him, she had an irrepressible urge to rush at him, leap into his massive arms and attack his perfect mouth.

It'd been like that for the past seven years.

Oh, who was she kidding? More like ten.

As the male she danced with moved around her, Mal's gaze slid to the female who sat beside Xavier at the bar. Blond, petite and quietly appealing. *Why does Xavier have to go for the exact opposite of me?* she screamed silently, wondering if it was psycho to actually plot the woman's death while dancing with some random guy.

Then Xavier reached across the top of the bar and covered the woman's hand.

A shock of pain brought Mal's head around. Her gaze connected with Beau and his dark eyes and dreamy smile. "I need another drink."

He grinned. "I'll get it for you, darlin'. Just stay here and keep those hips swayin' and those hands runnin' up and down yourself. I'll be right back."

Why couldn't Xavier say things like that? Well, maybe not exactly like that. Maybe not so creepy and proprietary, but something that indicated that he saw her as a female and not his best friend's little sister?

She closed her eyes and moved seductively to the music. She felt someone come up behind her, definitely male, maybe Beau, maybe not, but she didn't stop to look. Tonight and for the next three nights, she just wanted to let go, give in, feel, be felt…

***

She needed a spanking.

Maybe more than one.

Xavier narrowed his eyes on the Hunter female who was gyrating on the makeshift dance floor, sandwiched between two greasy human males, while another ordered drinks a few feet down the bar. Did he blame them for going after her? Leering at her? Drooling like dogs? No, he did not. With her perfect body clad in way-too-tight clothes, hungry green eyes, and thick ebony hair flowing down her back, she looked like a goddamn sex kitten tonight, and he was going to pummel the bastard who'd let her out of her cage.

Where the fuck was Aristide?

Her brother—and Xavier's closest friend—never let his sister out of his sight, except when she worked as a Hunter. And even then, Xavier could count on the rest of the Pantera to watch her. They all knew how special she was. Important. The kind of female you put up on a pedestal and stared at.

Not fucking leered at.

His eyes narrowed into pinprick slits as he watched her rock the dance floor. How the hell had she learned to move like that? Her hips. Her ass. Her hands threading in her hair and running down her body.

Another jolt moved through him, but he forced it away. He always forced away those kinds of flashes when it came to her. Amalie was not just the last Pantera born, which made her untouchable in and of itself, but she was also his best friend's little sister. And the code of honor between males killed even the most desperate of attractions.

He stood, slipped the flash drive the woman beside him had brought with her into his jeans pocket. "You didn't have to disable the camera to get these shots, did you?"

The blond PI he'd hired to help in his search for Ashe and Isi's father, Chayton, shook her head. "No. But it was a bitch and a half to get up there, and *stay* up there while I located the serial number. Thank god some asshole got a tattoo last night. Gave me a solid hour."

The human female had found a hidden camera in Isi's voodoo shop, and had spent the past three days trying to get a few minutes alone with it. "Did you run the number?"

"It's some exclusive, expensive shit. There's a list of the high-end stores that sell cameras like that on your drive, but I couldn't get sales records. You're going to need a top notch hacker."

Good thing he was one, Xavier thought, his gaze sliding over to the dance floor again. A growl sounded in his throat. Amalie was grinding her hips against some human male like she wanted sex.

"My payment?" the PI said.

"Already in your account."

She laughed softly, almost seductively. "Gotta love a man who anticipates a woman's needs. Can I buy you a drink?"

"Not tonight," he said, his eyes still pinned to the Hunter female and the human drooling machines bracketing her. "But I'll be in touch."

He pushed away from the bar and headed through the small crowd to the dance floor. He should be gone by now, heading back to Geek headquarters, checking out the drive the PI had just handed him. After all, it was vital the Pantera find Chayton before their enemies did.

A good fifteen patrons were working it to the killer baseline of some rapper, and a few females tried to catch Xavier's eye and draw him into their circle. But he only had eyes for one female, and she was going back to the Wildlands immediately. To her home, and to her brother's care.

Eyes closed, full pink lips parted, long hair mussed, the female before him looked like she'd just come from her bed. Xavier drew close and wrapped his large hand around her slim wrist. Instantly, her eyes opened. At first, she seemed confused as she stared up at him. Then, as she registered not only his presence but his hold on her, she smiled.

"Hi, Xavier," she said. "Want to join the party?"

Shit. How many drinks had she had? Her speech wasn't slurred, but it was pretty damn close. "You're making a scene, Amalie."

"My name is Mal," she corrected him, her luscious jade-green eyes flashing momentary fire. "And I'm not making a scene, I'm having fun."

Three or four drinks of fun. He didn't say a word, just lowered his hand to close around hers and led her off the dance floor. Xavier knew she could fight him if she wanted to. The female was tough as hell. Smart, too. But she didn't. In fact, she squeezed his hand and moved with him through the crowd and toward the door. Maybe it was the alcohol in her blood? Could do funny things to the Pantera system.

113

Night was just settling in, but the warm bayou air of the day still remained, rushing over Xavier's skin as he stepped outside. As he turned Amalie to face him, his hands on her shoulders, he tried not to stare at how that same breeze affected her hair, sending it swirling about her face.

Her fucking perfect face.

Releasing her and sliding his gaze away, Xavier growled low in his throat. Thoughts like these were becoming too commonplace lately. He needed to find a way to get rid of them. Permanently. Or he'd have to get rid of himself being around this female, permanently.

Amalie cocked her head. "Are you growling at me, Xavier?" Her tone was all flirtation, warmth, intimacy. "Not that I'm complaining."

"How much have you had to drink?" he said tightly.

"Not nearly enough."

"Your Pantera scent is being strangled by tequila."

She shrugged. "Shit happens."

"Yes, it does," he said, moving closer to her. "Like you being here of all places. Does Aristide know you're here?"

Her eyes clouded over, and for a moment she just stared at him. Then she laughed and shook her head. "No, my jailer of a brother doesn't know I'm here. He's stuck in quarantine with that human woman, Ashe's sister."

Isi? The one whose blood had both damaged the Wildlands and had caused it to bring forth life?

And Aristide didn't tell me?

What the hell? Xavier mused darkly. Someone needed to be watching out for Amalie.

The door to The Cougar's Den burst open and one of Amalie's dance partners nearly stumbled out. When the greasy male spotted her, he grinned like a fucking wolf with prey in sight.

"You coming back in, darlin'?" he drawled.

"No," Xavier answered.

Amalie turned to give him a dirty look, then glanced back up at the human male. "In a minute, Beau."

Xavier growled at her. "I'm taking you home, Amalie."

Her gaze slid his way once again, and no longer was there even a hint of flirtation glittering there. "No, you're not. I'm here to have some fun. Just because you don't know the meaning of that word."

"I'll show you some fun," Beau said, loping down the steps toward them.

"I suggest you go back inside, Male," Xavier said darkly, though his gaze remained pinned to Mal. "We're leaving, Amalie. Say goodbye to your little friend here. Perhaps you can schedule a playdate for another day."

"Do you hear yourself?" she growled back at him. "I do."

She stuck a finger in his face. "I'm not the young cub you and Aristide get to tell what to do anymore. I'm a grown female."

Xavier sighed, his nostrils flaring with irritation. Yes, unfortunately, she was. A female with curves

115

designed to make a male anxious to breed. A face angels would be envious of. A husky voice that belonged near a hungry male's ear.

All attributes that shouldn't be allowed near this oily, drunken human.

"Say goodbye, Amalie," he said evenly.

"She doesn't want to say goodbye," Beau said with a grunt. "Do you, Amalie?"

"My name's Mal," she corrected.

Beau chuckled, his eyes pinned to her chest. "Hey, I'll call you whatever you want, Sexy."

"Oh, I like that." Amalie's gaze flickered Xavier's way, and she said something under her breath that sounded an awful lot like, "Why can't you ever call me that?"

Xavier pretended not to hear her. Just as he pretended to not be affected by the way she chewed her lower lip. He shook his head slowly. "You know I can't let this happen, Amalie."

Her hands went to her hips. "The funny part is that you actually believe that. Or is the funny part that you're still doing Aristide's job? I'm not sure. Wait. Maybe they're both funny."

The human moved closer to her, his eyes now trained on her ass. "I know some funny stories, Mal. I'll buy you a drink and share a few."

Xavier felt his insides flood with aggression. This male was about two seconds away from unconsciousness. Which would be a bad idea, as they were on human land. The last thing Pantera wanted to do was draw attention to themselves. But this idiot was really begging for it.

"I'm going to say this once more, *mon ami*." Xavier's eyes narrowed on the human male. He wasn't particularly tall, but what he lacked in height, he made up for with muscle. Not Pantera kind of muscle, but impressive for a human. Something to consider if things went bruised and bloody. "Go inside and find yourself another female. This one is not available."

"I'll decide if I'm available or not," Amalie said tightly. "You got some nerve, Xavier. Go home."

The human grinned, then slid his arm around Amalie's waist, yanked her close and licked the curve of her ear. "You tell him, Sexy."

The haze that had only a second ago glimmered in Amalie's smoky green eyes receded, and a flare of golden heat took its place. It was the sign her cat hovered at the surface of her skin. Her control was lost, courtesy of too much tequila. In under five seconds, she removed the male's arm from her waist, took his hand in hers and slammed it back into his face. Making a sound like air escaping a balloon, Beau slithered to the ground and remained.

Xavier's eyes flipped up to meet hers. "Was that necessary?"

She stumbled backwards a step. "He licked me."

"Grow up, Amalie."

"You won't let me." Her eyes locked to him. "You and Aristide."

Xavier's gut clenched. She had no idea how he saw her, how his skin ached every time she touched him – how he stood taller, prouder, every time her eyes were on him. And hell, she never would, if he could manage it.

"Then perhaps we should concentrate on sobering up." He reached for her hand. "We're leaving. Now."

She didn't try to pull away. "Careful, Puma. Or I'll drop you like I dropped Tongue-Boy there."

Xavier refused to reply to such absurdity. As he moved past her, he scooped her up in his arms and continued down the path toward the parking lot.

"Neanderthal," she spat out.

"Pantera," he corrected, trying not to think about how good she felt in his arms. How right. How natural.

"You don't have to carry me," she grumbled. "I know how to use my legs."

His jaw went tight at her words. So did everything below his waist. Fucking female. Fucking male brain for taking those innocent words and twisting them into a goddamn fantasy. "It'll take us all night to walk home," he said. "And something tells me you can't run in those come-fuck-me-boots."

She glanced up at him. "Is that what they're called?"

He didn't answer, didn't look at her either. She'd been too goddamn beautiful in the harsh fluorescent lights of the club. Under the glow of twilight, he was pretty sure she'd send certain parts of his anatomy skyward.

He didn't need that. Not tonight. Not ever.

Clearing the parking lot, he took off toward the dark protection of the woods. He was fast in his human state, but he ached to shift to his puma and really taste the wind.

"So, I guess you're my way home tonight," she said with a soft yawn.

His arms tightened around her. "Who brought you? How did you get to The Den?"

"I caught a ride."

"If you tell me with a stranger—" he began through gritted teeth.

He felt her shrug. "He was only a stranger for the first five minutes."

A low growl escaped his throat. Shit, he needed to break out the fur and the canines. "I'm going to take you home and tie you up until Aristide gets out of quarantine."

She snorted, then yawned again. "I'd like to see you try."

"Would you?"

He made the mistake of looking down at her. Trying to put the sweet weight of her body out of his mind as he moved was problem enough. Now he saw full lips, drowsy eyes, a strip of tanned stomach where her tank was riding up.

Fuck. Me.

"What about your date?" she said. "Isn't she waiting back at The Den for you?"

"That was business."

She snorted softly. "She didn't look like business. She looked like she wanted to do some licking of her own."

Xavier growled—not at the idea of the human PI, but with the recent memory of that greasy human male's hands on Amalie. His *tongue* on Amalie.

"What?" she asked, concern lacing her tone.

"If I didn't have to babysit you tonight, I'd go back to The Cougar's Den, scrape the human male up off the ground and remove his eager tongue from his mouth."

"I took care of it, Xavier."

"Yes. And you provoked it. Humans should not be played with. It's not good for us."

"Us or me?" she said softly.

Xavier didn't answer. Doing so would mean he'd have to examine his feelings for his best friend's sister. And he made it a practice never to do that. Instead, he picked up speed, racing through the bayou lands toward the border. Quiet, except for the sound of the breeze and the buzzing of the insects, reigned. Xavier had actually thought Amalie asleep when she moved in his arms and spoke.

"Xavier?"

Goddamn, her soft, yet husky voice wrapped around him. Squeezed the shit out of him. "Yeah?"

"When we get to the edge of the Wildlands…I don't think I can shift."

"The tequila?"

She nodded against his chest. "Sorry."

With a soft, protective growl, he pulled her closer to his chest. "Not to worry, Amalie. I'll carry you to the border, and my puma will carry you home."

CHAPTER TWO

The moon's filtered light followed them as they traveled the varied terrain of the Wildlands. Night was in full bloom now, bringing with it cool air and rich, earthy scents. Her arms wrapped around the thick neck of Xavier's cat, Mal reveled in the smooth cadence of his movement. She'd only ridden on the back of a puma once before. When she'd lodged a thorn in her foot after a hard-won race between a few Hunters last year. But it was nothing like this. Xavier's puma was not only large and powerful, it was quick and sharp and keen. And riding on his back, under the moonlight, seduced by the scents and the wind, made her wonder how it would feel to not only ride him, but to be ridden—

Her sensual thought was ripped from her mind as Xavier came to a halt in front of her small, sage green house. For a second, she just remained on his back, wondering why she hadn't noticed them entering the boundaries of town. Hadn't, at the very least, scented it.

She scrambled off of him, and, from the shelter of a rose-trellised archway, watched as he shifted from sleek black cat into devastatingly hot male. Her heart squeezed. Wearing jeans that stretched over heavily muscled thighs and a killer ass, and a black T-shirt that could barely contain his vast chest and bulging arms, Xavier made every female who came within a mile of him sigh. Tall, dark and fierce, he was sex walking. And added to it—Mal's favorite attribute of all—those incredible, icy blue eyes. Well, she just wanted to get lost in him and not be found for days.

If only he wanted that too.

Damn. Why couldn't he notice her? See her as the one female on earth who was perfect for him, would make him happy?

"Who's staying with you while Aristide is quarantined?" Xavier asked, following her up the path to her front door.

"No one."

He made a sound deep in his throat. It was a cross between a growl and a groan, and it made her insides flare with heat.

"Not acceptable, Amalie."

She glanced over her shoulder. "You realize I'm a grown female, right?"

His gaze, those shockingly blue eyes, traveled down her body. Then he looked away and hissed.

No. He didn't see her as grown.

Or wouldn't.

Irritation moving over and through her, she turned back and opened her front door with a hiss of her own. She was growing into quite the little masochist. Maybe it was time for that to stop.

She called over her shoulder, "Thanks for the ride."

But before she took a step inside, she felt him at her back, his massive frame pressed against her, his warm breath near her ear. "We're not done talking about this."

Without her permission, her skin went tight, and everything below her waist clenched. "I think I am. I'm tired and still a little drunk and I should probably go to bed."

"You can't stay here alone."

"Why not?"

He moved to her side, leaned against the doorframe. "It's not safe."

She laughed. "Are you serious? I'm a Hunter. Even you would be hard-pressed to get me on my back." When his eyes narrowed at her words, her laughter downgraded to an embarrassed chuckle. "You know, unless I wanted to be there."

His jaw tightened. "I know you can handle yourself physically, Amalie. What concerns me is shit like tonight."

"I went out and had fun like a bunch of other people do every damn day. What's the problem?"

"You had too much to drink and it affected your judgment."

Her judgment? She snorted. Shit, that had been compromised ten years ago when she'd seen Xavier with his shirt off for the first time. Summer on the bayou. Warm water, warmer evenings. Swim party for her birthday, and Xavier—the most perfect birthday present ever—came to hang out with Aristide. Of course, he hadn't even looked her way. Mal didn't

123

even think he'd known it was her birthday. But she'd noticed him. Back then and every day since.

"My judgment is fine," she told him. "I won't drink as much next time, that's all."

He shook his head. "There's not going to be a next time."

She glared at him. Crush of a lifetime or not, Xavier was being a pain in the ass, aka a wannabe substitute for her brother. And that she wasn't going to put up with.

"Okay, we're done here. I'm going to bed." She pushed past him into the house, and stalked into the foyer. "Just lock the door before you take off. You know, so I stay safe and all."

Ten years, she grumbled. Ten freaking years she'd spent internally—and probably externally as well—swooning for this male, and he either couldn't see her as anything but Aristide's sister, or just didn't find her attractive. Ugh, that last bit stung, and she wondered how much longer this feeling, this need, was going to lay claim to her heart. Maybe she should make another trip into town. Not to The Cougar's Den, this time, but to that Voodoun's shop. Maybe inquire about a potion to kill her crush.

Feeling a rush of alcohol-infused heat take over her skin, she pulled off her tank and dropped it on the floor of the hall as she headed toward her bedroom. *Tomorrow. Tomorrow when she sobered up she was going to stop wanting the ridiculously beautiful Geek.*

She got halfway to her bedroom before a shocking smack of dizziness hit her. Stars glittered in front of her eyes, and she cursed and reached out for the wall. When her hands met nothing but air, panic gripped her heart. Then the floor rushed up to meet her, and her vision went utterly black.

***

Xavier's heart dropped into his balls as he caught Amalie before she hit the floor.

Christ, this female made him crazy, he growled inwardly, settling her into his arms. Flirting with him one second, pissed off at him the next. He pulled her close as he moved down the hallway. Yes, he knew she liked him. Had this lighthearted crush on him. And he'd be lying his ass off if he didn't admit to having his own attraction and problematic curiosity about her...how she might taste, how her skin smelled...

Fuck. He was going to hell. Or the Pantera equivalent: down beneath the Wildlands, imprisoned with Shakpi.

He was never going to act on that attraction. She was Aristide's blood, precious to the Pantera, completely off-limits.

Entering her bedroom, Xavier couldn't help but glance around as he made a beeline for the bed. Shit, the female acted so tough, but when it came down to it, she was all heart and fluffy white bedspreads and flowered pillows. Hard on the outside, soft and sweet on the inside. His insides curled with desire at the thought.

Why did he find that juxtaposition so damned sexy?

With gentle hands, he placed her on the cool, white blanket, then sat down next to her. His gaze raked over her face. *What a fucking vision.* Dappled moonlight streamed in through the window to his right, spotlighting her yards of rich, dark hair, beautiful face, pink mouth and long, supple neck. His traitorous gaze moved downward. The tank was gone, now a small, white puddle forgotten in the hallway. All she had on was a bra, and a skimpy one at that. And the creamy slip of lacy fabric barely covered her large breasts.

His mouth watered.

Rein it in, asshole.

The lids of her eyes moved, and she fisted one hand and moaned.

Xavier leaned in and brushed a strand of hair off her pale cheek. Trying not to focus on how soft her skin felt under the rough pads of his fingers, he whispered soothingly, "Everything's okay, Amalie. You're home. In your bed."

Her eyes fluttered open, and for a moment those smoky green orbs displayed extreme confusion. But in seconds, the haze dissipated, and she blinked, her teeth grazing her bottom lip. An action that once again had Xavier's skin tightening over his muscles.

"Xavier?"

He nodded. "How you feeling?"

She didn't answer him. Her eyes were pinned to his and her breathing grew labored.

"What?" he asked, concern moving through him. When she'd fallen, had he not caught her in time? Had she hurt herself? "What's wrong?"

"I'm not a cub."

Relief moved through him. This wasn't pain he was seeing in her eyes, but frustration. "I know you're not," he said.

"You all treat me like I am."

"No," he amended, his voice dark, quiet. "We treat you like you're special."

She flinched, then huffed out a breath and looked away, past him. "So I was the last cub born to the Pantera. Who cares? Why does that mean anything different than the second-to-last cub? Or the third? It doesn't make me special. It just makes me lucky."

Xavier didn't want to do this. Have this conversation. Especially not in her moonlit room, sitting on her bed. Granted, he understood the Pantera's affections and protective ways regarding Amalie, but his actions and reactions were less about her 'last born' status and more about his own barely controlled attraction. Truthfully, if she wasn't Aristide's sister, he wasn't all that sure he'd give a good goddamn about the Pantera's need to keep her sheltered.

"You should sleep now," he told her.

"I don't want to sleep." With a frustrated sigh, she came up on her elbows. "I want to be free. I want to live my own life. I want to be treated like something that can't be broken with just a simple touch."

"No touch is simple," Xavier said quietly. "Trust me."

"I don't want to trust you!" she suddenly exploded, sitting all the way up, tears welling in her eyes. "Goddamit!" She threw up her hands. "I want to know it myself! I want to feel it myself!"

"Amalie—"

"I'm a fucking grown female!" she cried, looking down.

"I know."

Her eyes snapped up to meet his. "Do you?"

His breath caught in his lungs. As much as she was beautiful when she was docile and flirtatious, she was nearly irresistible like this. So impassioned, so vicious, like she wanted to kiss the shit out of him, then knee him in the balls.

His gaze moved over her face, down the smooth column of her neck, then into her spectacular cleavage. Did he know she was a grown female?

Fuck yeah.

"Listen to me, Xavier," she fairly growled. "If I don't get *broken* soon, I'm going to lose my mind."

"Don't talk like that," he growled back, giving her a fierce look, his cock twitching.

"Why not? It's true. There's nothing wrong with wanting to be touched, wanting to go out and have a good time. Wanting sex."

Christ, she was killing him. "I'm warning you, Amalie—"

"Just because you don't see me as a grown female doesn't mean other males don't."

"No males will be getting within ten feet of you," he declared roughly.

"You can't say shit like that."

"I just did." He stood up. He had to rearrange. He had to get the hell out of this room, out of her airspace before he did something regrettable.

She looked up at him, her eyes deep and dark, her hair wild and falling over her shoulders and between her breasts. "Go home, Xavier."

He should. He really should.

In fact, he should walk out of this house and never come back. From now on, he and Aristide would meet somewhere else, anywhere else. And when Amalie's name was brought up, he'd pray for deafness.

Instead, he narrowed his eyes on the half-naked vixen sitting in a pool of white softness before him and said with deadly calm, "I'm not going anywhere."

One dark eyebrow raised. "*Pardonnez-moi?*"

"Clearly you can't be trusted on your own." He turned and headed for the door, calling over his shoulder, "While Aristide is gone, I'll be taking care of you."

CHAPTER THREE

Bastard.

Asshole.

God, she wanted to jump him.

Mal stared, watched Xavier's exit with hungry, greedy eyes. He looked so good from behind. Even if he was walking away from her.

With a sigh of self-disgust, she dropped back on the pillow and closed her eyes. Truly, it stung that Xavier was staying with her out of obligation—not out of want. Or desire. She'd thought, fantasized, about being alone with him for so long, and now here they were. Not making out as she'd hoped, but residing in two separate rooms, both clothed, both breathing normally, skin not coated in a thin layer of sweat...

She groaned and turned on her side.

And yet, no matter the reason, he *was* staying.

For three days and three nights.

She wrapped herself around her extra-long pillow and squeezed, a glimmer of something akin to hope and wonder moving through her blood. In her mind, she saw him. Emerging from the bayou, his beautiful brown skin wet, his muscles flexing, his dangerous blue eyes catching hers as he stepped onto the bank.

Naked.

Her skin hummed, and she grinned as old memories and new fantasies collided. She wanted to release this long-held need she had for him, but it just clung so tightly to her. He was perfect. The body of a Hunter, the heart of a Nurturer and the brains of a Geek. He was everything she'd ever wanted.

Well, with one exception.

He refused to see her as grown or sexual or even female.

I'll be taking care of you.

Her breasts tightened at just the memory of his deep, husky promise, and between her thighs, heat radiated. She was a strong female, passionate, and a truly capable Hunter. Rarely did she lose the prey she sought. And damn, she sought Xavier something fierce. She wanted his touch to be her first. Obligation or not, she'd already 'captured' him. Now she just had to make her gorgeous prey see what was right in front of him.

Hugging her pillow close, she drifted off to sleep with a confident, hungry smile.

***

I'm @ clinic. Quarantined w/Ashe's sister. Her blood being tested. Take care of Mal 4 me. 3-4 days, they think. Thx, mon ami. I owe u.

Seated on the couch in Aristide and Amalie's living room, two of his laptops open on the coffee table in front of him, Xavier read the text from his best friend again. The text he hadn't even known he'd gotten until one of his Geeks dropped off his phone, along with his laptops, at the house a few hours ago. The thing screamed at him. Gave him the finger. Threatened him with pitchforks, torches and the sharpened claws of a pissed off puma brother.

Goddammit.

Take care of her? Shit, it was like asking a forest fire to take care of a pile of dry brush. But he'd do it. Hell yes, he'd do it. Aristide was his best friend, true, but he was also family. It was Aristide and Amalie's parents who had helped Xavier's mother find her smile again after his father's death. The two Nurturers had always been there for him. For advice, a meal, a place to crash when he was being a hardheaded cub and his mom couldn't handle him. And he wouldn't betray them. Not with their own daughter, for fuck's sake.

His eyes slid to the screen on his right. Along with photos of Isi's shop, photos of the camera from several different angles and close-ups on the serial number, there was a list of high-end camera shops within a ninety miles radius that carried the model. For the past few hours, he'd been working the web on his second computer, seeing if any of the images from the camera had been uploaded. Then he could backtrack, searching the serial numbers embedded in the jpegs. But so far he hadn't had any luck. Looked like he was going to have to go through the records of each camera store.

His phone rang, and for a second he thought it might be Aristide. But one glance at the readout and he saw that the call wasn't coming from the clinic, but from Geek central.

"Xavier."

"You get anything?" Robby asked. The male Geek had started off as Hunter, but he'd quickly found his home with the other tech heads. Even took on the screen name "Robin Hood" because he was all about stealing information if it helped someone in trouble.

"Not yet," Xavier told him. "Going to have to do a little breaking and entering."

"Mmm, my favorite," he said. "Send me some, I've got a few hours to kill before bed."

"No. I'm going to bring Captain in on this one. I have another job for you."

"I'm not bringing you pajamas, so don't even ask."

Xavier snorted. "Not necessary. First off, because I don't wear them and second, because Danny brought me everything I need."

"Too much info, bro. The first part."

Chuckling, Xavier explained, "I need you to hack into the computer at Isi's shop, The Care and Feeding of Voodoo."

"Nice name."

"Don't start hatin', *Robin Hood*."

"Fuck you."

Xavier laughed.

"So, what do you want me to look for, bro?"

"Anything on the computer about Chayton, anything in her emails. Any correspondence with people who have interest in Chayton, or finding her father. Do the store's website, too. Any posts, questions, comments, that type of thing."

"You got it."

"I'm sure she has some kind of firewall up."

Robby laughed, said arrogantly, "Please."

"Take it down in under ten seconds and I'll let you stay on the Geek squad."

"Under five and I'm the new leader," Robby countered.

"Keep dreaming, bro." Staring at the screen, Xavier sobered. "I'm just afraid this guy's gone completely off the grid."

"Everyone's got a footprint, X. You know that."

"Well, lets hope so. I'll talk to you later."

"It is later, bro," Hood said with a grin in his voice before he hit the end button and killed the connection.

Tossing his cell onto the couch cushions, Xavier glanced at the time on the top of his screen. Five in the morning. Shit, he hadn't realized how long he'd been at it. Going hard and heavy for five hours straight. Maybe he needed a break. Maybe he needed a drink. Damn, maybe he needed...

Before the thought cleared his brain, his nostrils flared, scenting her arrival seconds before he heard her.

"What's all this?" Amalie said, moving toward him.

Xavier's entire body flared with heat, but he didn't acknowledge her presence until he closed both computers. "Work."

"More with the human woman?" she asked, her tone only mildly curious as she walked around the side of the couch.

"No, this cybertracking job was a solo all-nighter—"

The words died in his throat, and he inhaled sharply. *What the hell*—

His breath came out in a rush, and before he could stop it, his puma broke from his control and blazed to the surface of his skin. His hands balled into fists. His mind screamed at the cat to retreat. Never in his life had he experienced such a reaction. Such a wild, instinctual response. To anything or anyone. He didn't understand it, and quickly forced it back down, beneath his pounding heart where it belonged.

Panting, his eyes raked over the female standing in front of him. "What the hell are you wearing?"

"A towel." She looked at him like he was crazy. "And was that your puma I just saw? Flashing in and out of your features?"

He shook his head. No. That wasn't possible. He didn't do the uncontrolled cat thing. "I'm just tired, that's all."

"Then maybe you should get some sleep." She gestured down the hall, which meant she released the front of her towel with one hand.

Thank fuck she had two.

"Aristide's bed is available," she said, her dark eyes glistening. "And mine too, if you'd be more comfortable in a clean and fresh-smelling environment."

It had been said with halfhearted humor, but once again, the puma inside him rushed upward, flaring to life. What the hell was going on? He glared at Amalie, praying she and her barely clothed self weren't the

135

cause. Hoping it was truly lack of sleep and maybe lack of food that was making him so edgy.

"Why are you in that goddamn towel?" he ground out.

She cocked her head. "Shower."

"In the living room?" he countered blackly. "Are you trying to make me crazy?"

Her brows lifted and a smile played about her lips. "Why? Would it work?"

"I'm male, Amalie. And you're..." His gaze traveled over her and he growled.

"I'm what?" she encouraged.

His eyes narrowed. "A devious brat."

She laughed. The sound pierced his skin and went straight to his groin.

"Shower's outside the house remember?" she said.

"Right." Goddammit. So, this was going to be a regular thing over the next three days? Showering? The untouchable goddess walking around in skimpy towels, making him drool and growl and hunger for things other than food?

"I'm on patrol in an hour," she said. "Better get soaped up."

Stay the hell down, he warned his puma. "Next time wear a robe," he said as she started past him.

She paused, gave him a lopsided smile. "Why?"

"You know why, Amalie." His tone was like ice. Ice that wanted to be melted in a hot shower with a hotter female.

"You see me as family, right?" she challenged. "So what's the problem?"

He turned back to his laptops and opened them. "Go. Take your shower. Get to work."

She chuckled. "Have a good day, Xavier."

"Yeah, you too," he muttered to himself.

But she heard him, and called over her shoulder, "Oh, I will."

Xavier told himself not to turn, not to look, not to watch her move down the hall in that goddamn scrap of white cotton, but it was impossible. Like iron to a magnet, he ripped his eyes from the screen and glanced over his shoulder. With flared nostrils and a tight chest, he watched as her towel slipped down her back to her hips as she sauntered away, giving him a view of her back and the rise of her ass.

This time when his puma rushed to the surface of his skin, he let it.

CHAPTER FOUR

The sun was high in the sky as Mal sprinted along the west border, every so often opening her mouth to taste the air.

It remained.

Always remained.

The sour stench of human intruders. Problem was she couldn't find the source. She and her partner had been patrolling for six hours straight—and nothing.

Hiss came to an abrupt halt near the footbridge that curved over the small stream that jutted out from the bayou. With a shake of his auburn pelt, he shifted from cat to human male.

Coming up beside him, Mal shifted too. "What? Did you scent something?"

The rugged male Hunter, who wore his dark hair back in a leather thong, shook his head. "It's the same everywhere we go. Dying land, sour stench, but no clues. No intruders. I don't get it."

"They'll be back. Both human, and any more traitors we harbor." She gave him a tight grin. "Damn, I'd love to be the one who catches that prey."

Hiss's grey eyes flashed. "You and me both."

"I wonder if they're camping far enough outside the border to keep their scent quiet." Releasing a heavy breath, Mal shaded her eyes and looked out over the quiet bayou water. "Maybe we should go take a look."

A wide grin split the male's handsome features. "Go hunting across the border?"

"Maybe."

"Those aren't our orders."

She matched his grin and shrugged. "So?"

He laughed. "I like patrolling with you, Mal. Taking risks is important for a Hunter. Keeps us sharp. Keeps our instincts—"

"Oh my god!" Mal exclaimed, cutting him off, her attention suddenly diverted by something she saw out of the corner of her eye.

"What?" Hiss said, alert now. "What is it? Humans?"

Her eyes nearly bugging out of her head, Mal ran to the edge of bayou and waded a foot into the water. "Look."

Hiss followed her, shading his eyes as he searched the calm surface for whatever she was indicating. When his breath caught in his throat, Mal knew he'd seen it, too.

"I…I didn't think…" Hiss stumbled over his words. "*Merde*…with everything that's happened. With Ashe's sister, and her strange effects on the land…I didn't think we'd see it this year. I didn't think we'd see it ever again. What a miracle."

Her face growing warm with happiness and pleasure, Mal waded in deeper until she was forced to swim. Her clothes felt heavy in the water, but she didn't care. She couldn't believe it. She had to touch it.

"*Mon dieu*, do you scent it?" Hiss called from the bank.

Mal didn't answer. She was upon it now, its heady fragrance slamming into her nostrils. It made her insides vibrate, and her outsides, too. She reached out, palmed the large water lily that had only a moment ago been as white as the clouds overhead. Now, it was pale lavender, the color growing deeper and more vibrant with every moment that passed. She couldn't speak, she was smiling too hard.

The most perfect Dyesse Lily she had ever seen.

Even though they knew it was the time of year for the Dyesse Fete, they had all been secretly praying the celebration of the birth of the Pantera—and the most important holiday in the Wildlands—would actually come to pass. With the land's magic deteriorating at such a rapid rate, they'd wondered if any would remain.

Especially something so powerful and rare as the Dyesse.

She released the lily, and as she did, the two bracketing it started to change. By tonight, even the moon would turn a shockingly beautiful shade of violet. Laughing with unabashed happiness, she turned back to Hiss on the shore, and a silent understanding passed between them.

"I'm going right now," he called. "I'll tell Parish."

She swam toward him with fast, powerful strokes, hit the shore just as he shifted into his puma and growled his excitement. She did the same, shaking off the excess water that had transferred from her skin to the fur of her puma.

Hiss spoke inside her head. *You want to go with me?*

She looked up, growled. *To the fete?*

His puma nodded, smoky-grey eyes flashing with enthusiasm. *Good food, music, sparring matches. We were the first to spot the change. It's only right we celebrate together.*

Hiss was a friend, nothing more, but she liked him, felt comfortable with him, and god, it felt good to be asked. And, she thought with wicked intent, maybe good for Xavier to see. A grown male, a Hunter, wanted to take her to the most important night of the year for the Pantera—the night when unbridled mating was encouraged.

She grinned at the auburn cat. *Okay.*

Great! I'll pick you up around seven.

He turned and darted off into the forest, and Mal glanced over her shoulder, crying out into the fragrant air as she saw yards of Dyesse lilies turn purple on the calm surface of the bayou.

***

"I don't want to see him, Jax," Xavier said with an irritated growl. "I just want to talk to him."

The male guarding the door leading to the quarantine barracks shook his head. "Sorry, *mon ami.*"

"Look, the male's a good friend. I'm watching his house, his sister." A soft snarl accompanied that last word. Xavier ignored it. "I need a word."

"Can't help you. There's no outside communication unless this is an emergency." The male raised a pale blond brow. "Is this an emergency?"

Fuck. "No. It's not." He released a frustrated breath. "Fine. I'll see him in a couple of days."

"That's only an estimate," Jax said with a thin-lipped smile. "Could be a week. We just don't know."

Perfect. The news just got better and better, Xavier thought darkly. And more problematic. Three days under the same roof as that towel-wearing puma temptress was bad enough. How the hell was he going to last a week?

He gave the guard a curt nod, then turned and headed back down the hall. Maybe he could get someone else to watch her? One of the grandmothers... A low chuckle exited his throat. Yeah, that would go over well. She barely tolerated him. She'd make quick work of some sweet, old Pantera female.

"Hey, X."

Lost in thought, Xavier turned to see Raphael a few feet away. The leader of the Suits looked pretty shredded, like he hadn't slept in weeks, and was standing outside his mate, Ashe's, room, with a small group: Hunter leader Parish, Nurturer Jean-Baptiste and his mate, Genevieve, who Xavier knew from her momentary blip with the Geeks. They all turned to acknowledge him.

"Checking in on Aristide?" Jean-Baptiste asked. Being from the same faction, the Nurturer knew that Xavier and Aristide were tight.

"Something like that," Xavier said. Not keen on giving out details about his problem with Amalie, he quickly turned from the heavily tatted male to Raphael and changed the subject. "How is she? Your mate?"

The Suit's jaw went tight and he slid his green gaze toward the closed door. "She was better when her sister was around."

"The quarantine?" Xavier asked.

Raphael nodded.

Yeah, that thing was fucking with everyone's lives.

"But I'm hoping I can take her out for awhile," the Suit said. "Take her to the fete tonight."

"The fete?" Xavier repeated, momentarily stunned. He looked from Raphael to Parish. "Has there been a sighting?"

Parish nodded, his gold eyes flashing, his face splitting into a wide grin. "Two of my Hunters spotted a bayou of purple lilies about thirty minutes ago."

Amazing, Xavier mused. *And wonderful*. He'd been wondering if the Dyesse would occur this year. It had been a hope on everyone's mind.

"Can't wait to take Julia," Parish said with a growl. "Celebrate our fertility right."

Leaning against Jean-Baptiste's side, Genevieve laughed. "I'd be careful. Females, even humans ones I imagine, can be overly demanding on the Dyesse Eve."

Parish grinned wickedly. "I look forward to being chased and caught by my Doc."

"Are you ready to run, my love?" Genevieve asked her male with a teasing grin.

143

Growling, pulling the blond female closer to his side, Jean-Baptiste nuzzled her cheek. "I will never run from you, Genny. It's time wasted when you could be ravishing the shit out of me."

Everyone laughed, even Raphael. It was good to see, Xavier mused. The ghost of a male letting down his guard. But it didn't last long. He turned his weary gaze back on Xavier.

"I know you met with the PI. Did she have something of interest? How are things progressing with Chayton? Any leads?"

Though most of the Pantera knew about their search for Ashe and Isi's father, it was the Suit leader who Xavier was reporting to. The male had become the reluctant go-between for the elders.

"I went through a shitload of sales records today from several different camera shops," he said with a snarl of frustration. "I want to figure out where this camera came from and who put it there. I don't think it was our enemies or human tattoo artist, Derek." He shook his head. "But you know me, whoever it is, I'll get them."

Raphael cuffed him on the arm. "I know you will. And hopefully it will lead us to Chayton."

Just then, the door beside Raphael opened and Parish's mate, Dr. Julia, poked her head out. "She's asking for you, Raphael."

Instantly alert, Raphael gave them a quick nod. "See you later. We should all take the night off and celebrate our birth, and the magic that continues within us despite those who are trying to destroy it." He eyed Xavier. "Even you, X."

As Raphael disappeared inside the room of his mate, Xavier and the rest of the group offered quick goodbyes before disbanding. Walking down the hall toward the front doors, Xavier thought about the Suit's words. A night off to celebrate the birth of his kind. He wanted that. Wanted to be a part of that. But time was ticking away. He had to find out who had placed that camera, and he had to find Chayton before those assholes did. Before they found him and used him to wake Shakpi.

If Xavier did his job right, there would be many more purple moons to celebrate.

CHAPTER FIVE

Butterflies inside her stomach and ants crawling up her spine, Mal put the finishing touches on her makeup, then stood back and took a long, hard look at herself. Not bad. For a first attempt. Lipstick, eyeliner and mascara were definitely not her thing. In fact, she'd felt kind of clueless putting it on and had needed to use one of Xavier's computers to look up a tutorial on how to apply makeup without looking like a clown.

She grinned at herself.

Normally, she went all natural. The Hunter look: jeans, tank, boots, clean face, easy and ready to shift into her puma. But tonight, she really wanted to make some heads explode. Well, one head. One very gorgeous, very stubborn head.

She was just finishing up washing her hands when she heard the front door open. Her heart stuttered in her chest as she fumbled with the towel. This was it. The great reveal. Not only had she put on makeup, but her dark hair was brushed to a shine and hung down her back in gentle waves, and the ultra-feminine dress she wore didn't even remotely resemble Hunter gear.

"Honey, I'm home!" Xavier called, the dark humor in his tone obvious. "Where are you? I brought dinner. I'm warming it up." The mild crash of a pot hitting the stovetop rose above the sudden silence. Then, "Aristide said you don't cook, or you can't cook. I can't remember which."

With one last look in the mirror, she released the breath she'd been holding and opened the door to her room. She spotted Xavier right away. He was bent over the kitchen counter, staring at the screen of his computer, something heating up in a pot on the stove, a rugged blue flame shooting off sparks beneath it. She swallowed, smoothed the front of her dress and walked toward him.

"Which one is it?" Xavier called, still staring at the screen. "You can't cook or you don't?"

"Both," she said.

Courage, Female. You hunt bad guys and badass animal prey all damn day, and this male's reaction to your new look is making you sweat?

"But I won't be eating dinner," she added, moving toward him, her heart pounding in her chest. "Not here anyway."

"What are you talking about, Female?" he asked, tearing his gaze from the screen to look up.

When he did, when he saw her, when his eyes traveled from her shiny hair all the way down to her strappy sandals, a strange sound exited his lips. It was like a cross between a wheeze and a growl, and ended with a ferocious lip curl. She waited for him to say something, move. But he didn't. He just stood there, hands balling into fists, ice blue eyes turning frosty— and his puma vibrating beneath his skin.

Forcing her nerves aside, Mal strode toward him. "Puma got your tongue, Xavier?"

His gaze remained fixed on her as she moved. "What are you wearing?"

"That's the first thing you're saying to me? Seriously."

"Hell yes, seriously," he growled. "Deadly seriously."

She stopped directly in front of him and lifted her chin. "It's a dress, Xavier."

His nostrils flared and she felt his cat's heat radiate off his body. "And why are you wearing a dress?"

"I'm going out."

His lip curled, and he slowly shook his head. "You're not going anywhere. Not like that."

"Like what exactly? Dressed up? Looking hot?"

His eyes nearly bugged out of his head.

"I'll take that as a yes." She grinned, then turned in a slow circle in front of him. "I do look hot, right?"

His jaw was so tight, Mal thought it might shatter into a hundred pieces.

"Doesn't matter, Amalie," he said icily. "You're not going out. Not like that, and not alone."

She looked up at him through her lashes. Her curled and painted lashes. "I'm not going alone."

This time, he moved. Closed the distance between them in one stride. He was so tall, so broad. Fearsome and sexy. Why couldn't he just lift her up and plant a killer kiss on her eager lips? He was so goddamn frustrating. "I have a date."

"No." He said the single word without heat.

She cocked her head to the side and chewed her lower lip. "I'm not asking permission."

"Good, because you're not getting it."

Her gaze flickered past him, to the stove—to the raging blue flame. Something caught her eye; something bubbling out of control. "Your sauce, or whatever it is you're making, is burning."

Cursing, Xavier whirled around and rushed to the stovetop. Without thinking, he grabbed the handle of the pot, then cursed again when the metal burned his hand. He tossed the pot into the sink and slammed on the water.

Forgetting the irritation-slash-flirtation from a moment ago, Mal hurried to the sink and to his side. "Are you all right?"

"Fine," he growled, fisting his hand.

"Let me see it."

"It's nothing."

She grabbed his hand and forced his fingers open. "Stop being a stubborn ass." Angry red welts decorated his palm. "Let's get some cool water on it."

He didn't fight when she guided his hand under the faucet, but hissed when the water met his skin.

"You're mothering me, Amalie," he said on a growl. "I don't need it."

She looked up at him, met those crystal blue eyes that always made her weak. "Welcome to my world, Friend."

He snarled gently. "Last thing I'm trying to do is mother you."

"Then what is it? This thing you're doing with me?"

His nostrils flared as he stared down at her, and once again, she felt heat roll off him. Why couldn't he say it, she thought angrily. Why couldn't he admit there was something inside him that wanted to reach out and touch her?

"I could make this cub go away, Amalie," he said, his eyes on her mouth now.

"He's not a cub. He's a grown male, a Hunter."

"Doesn't matter."

"Matters to me, Xavier. I deserve to celebrate this holiday like all the other Pantera. Maybe even more so, being the final birth."

That silenced him.

At least until the knock on the door.

His head came up, his eyes narrowed and he growled with unabashed antagonism.

"Okay, no." Amalie dropped his hand, which was already starting to heal, and pointed a finger at him. "You're not going to interrogate him or threaten him or whatever."

His eyes still pinned on the door, Xavier gave her a lazy shrug. "If he's a true Pantera male he won't have a problem with that."

She gave him a warning glare before hurrying to the door. As she opened it, she felt him come up behind her. *Damned puma. Damned mother hen.*

Standing on the porch in a pair of black jeans and a white dress shirt, looking far handsomer than she'd ever seen him, Hiss grinned at her. "Wow."

Mal grinned back. "Hey, Hiss."

His gray eyes moved over her. "You look beautiful, Hunter."

150

"Yes, she does," Xavier said, moving out from behind to stand beside her.

Mal rolled her eyes. "You know Xavier."

Hiss tore his gaze from Mal and acknowledged Xavier with a nod. "How's it going, X?"

"Great. You?"

"Fantastic. You going to the festival?"

Mal answered before Xavier had a chance. "No. He has to work."

Shrugging, grinning, Hiss said, "Too bad," then turned back to Mal. "Ready? Because that moon is turning violet as we stand here."

She nodded, then stepped out onto the porch. "Have a nice night, Xavier."

As they walked down the path, Mal glanced back over her shoulder. She probably shouldn't have, but as usual she couldn't stop herself when it came to looking at the gorgeous Geek. Her heart trembled with what she saw. Cast in the dark lavender light of the Pantera moon, Xavier looked severe and sexy. And ominous. And hungry. He was standing in the doorway, his massive frame barely allowing the light inside the house to peek through, his piercing blue eyes trained on her. Vehemence fairly radiated from him. As she turned and headed for town with Hiss, she prayed that envy was the emotion that sparked that look. And if it was, that Xavier might finally do something about it.

**

He was an idiot.
But it couldn't be helped.

The air circulating within the Wildlands was ripe and heady with the scent of purple water lily. A strange, yet addictive aroma. The Pantera's birth lily— the first flower to grow on their new land back when Opela created them—was purported to have a magical property that infused the Pantera in happiness, warmth and, for those who were mated or wished to be, a sensual euphoria.

Fine for most, Xavier mused, heading down the shop-lined street toward the center of town. But not the type of magic he wanted his wild little kitten exposed to.

Not unsupervised at any rate.

After she'd left, side by side with the Hunter, Xavier had gotten a call from Robby. The Geek had found a couple of interesting instant messages on Isi's store computer. At first, they'd reminded Xavier of poetry. But after several listens, he'd recognized the strange collection of words as protection spells, and had given Robby the go-ahead to follow that IM trail.

I should be working the keyboard too, he thought darkly. Not tracking and spying. Hanging out in the shadows of one of the town's many produce stands, scanning the Pantera's merriment for Amalie, making sure she acted sane—and that her Hunter male escort acted like a gentleman.

Deep in the shadows of the empty stand, Xavier let his gaze travel over the square. Given the limited amount of prep time, the Pantera had created quite a spectacle. Purple and lavender flowers and ribbons were everywhere, on tables, strung from tree to tree. In one corner, a Cajun band—five Suits who had played last year—was kicking up some fine, foot-stomping music. And warring with the scent of water lily, some of the species' best cooks were working over open flames, creating culinary magic and sending it out to the masses who were at tables, both long and intimate, around the wood floor that had been laid out for dancing. As usual, the food was being served family-style, passed around from table to table. Xavier's belly growled as he scented rich gumbos and crawfish, meat pies, vegetables, bread pudding and fruit. When he spotted his favorite, alligator sausage, he nearly howled.

But it was the sound of laughter—a female's laughter—over the din that made that sound truly exit his lips.

His eyes scanned the square, the diners, dancers, even a small group of shifted Pantera, who were sport fighting a yard or two away from the band. *Where are you, Female? I hear your laughter.* He didn't like that the male Hunter had caused such a reaction in her— had caused that beautiful face to break into the most infectious fucking smile in the world. No one should be making her laugh. No one, but—

Before he could finish with '*but me*' the music changed. From rocking bluegrass to a slow, Cajun waltz. As if the calming sound brought on another level of clarity to his vision, Xavier turned to see the pair at one of the small tables set apart from the others. They were standing up, their plates cleaned, and were heading for the dance floor. His hand clasping hers, the Hunter male led Amalie into the small crowd of couples and took her in his arms.

Xavier's body went rigid.

Sure, she deserved this night. And yes, she should have some fun. But why did it have to be with this male? This male who seemed like a decent guy, not like that slobbering dog back at The Cougar's Den. This male who acted respectful, and looked at her like he genuinely wanted to pursue something after tonight.

Amalie could actually like this male, he thought with a twist to his gut.

Shit, Aristide could like this male.

Without weighing the rights or wrongs of his actions, Xavier abandoned the shadows of the produce stand and headed toward the dance floor. He didn't want to be a prick. Didn't want to be a pushy bastard who claimed something he had no right to claim. But the desire to take Amalie from Hiss's arms was too strong to fight against.

Eyes pinned to them, Xavier moved easily and swiftly through the crowd. The song ended, and Hiss and Amalie were just stopping to clap when Xavier came up beside them.

"Mind if I cut in?" he said in the most forced polite voice in the world.

With a soft gasp, Amalie turned to look at him. Her eyes widened and she shook her head as if to say, 'Are you crazy?' He probably was, but he couldn't stop himself.

Hiss, however, grinned broadly. "Good to see you here, X. No one should be working tonight." Then he turned to Amalie. "I'll get us a couple of drinks, okay?"

"Thanks, Hiss," she said sweetly. But the moment the Hunter was out of earshot, she whirled on Xavier and spat out, "What are you doing here? Spying on me?"

"Yes."

She looked momentarily stunned by his honesty.

His eyes moved over her face and he closed the distance between them. "You look beautiful tonight." His arms went around her, and he started to move to the music. "Hot."

All the tension left her body and her face split into the most incredible smile he'd ever seen. "Thank you."

One dark eyebrow lifted as he amended, "Too hot."

Her mouth quirked. "Bastard."

He smiled and eased her closer. Her warm, soft skin beneath his palms, her gentle weight. She felt like heaven in his arms. And the scent of her mixed with the scent of purple water lily was acting like a drug on his control. Xavier's skin hummed with awareness, and in that moment there was nothing he wanted more than to pull her away from the crowd, ease her into the shadows where he'd once stood looking for her, and remove her pretty dress with his teeth.

Blood surged into his cock, making him hard.

No. Fuck, no. His mind was playing tricks. He couldn't have her. Not tonight. Not any night. But then again, neither could Hiss. He couldn't allow that either. No matter how nice and respectful the male was, no one else was going to touch her. He wouldn't allow it. Neither would his puma. A growl formed in his throat. The water lily's scent was capturing him, surely. What else could be the reason for these possessive thoughts?

"Come with me," he ordered, taking her by the hand and leading her off the dance floor.

"Talk about déjà vu," she said dryly. "Where are you going, Xavier? Hiss is coming back."

Ignoring her question, Xavier eased her into the shadows of the produce stand. Out of the corner of his eye, he saw Hiss, drinks in hand, searching the dance floor.

She isn't yours. Not now. Never ever.

Curling her around him, pressing her back to the faded-white walls of the stand, Xavier coiled over her and inhaled deeply.

Amalie stared up at him, her breathing labored. "What's wrong with you?"

Wrong? He nearly laughed. Shit, he was out of his mind. Drugged. Had to be. "I want to leave."

Irritation flashed in her green eyes and she made a move to get past him. "Then go."

But he placed a hand on either side of her and shook his head. "I want you to come with me."

She shook her head. "No."

"You got your touch," he whispered. "Your flirting. Your date."

"It's not enough. It's nothing. I want more."

A snarl escaped his throat and he leaned in close to her face, almost until they were nose to nose. "That Hunter touches you again and I'll hurt him."

Amalie growled at him and tried to back up, but there was nothing but wall. "What the hell is wrong with you?"

"I'm protecting you."

"From what? From Hiss? He's a good male."

"Don't say that."

"Then from what? Being held? Kissed? Those are normal things, Xavier."

His puma scratched to break free, and he nuzzled her nose with his own. "Dammit, Amalie."

"Come on, Xavier. Don't do this to me," she uttered, her tone pained. "Don't hold me, block me. It's not fair. Especially coming from you. Do you really expect me to go through life alone? Without being kissed? Staying a virgin—"

She never finished her thought. The word—no, the image—drove Xavier and his puma over the fucking edge. With a snarl of possession, he slid his thigh between her legs and covered her mouth with his own, kissing her long and hard and deep.

Oh, fuck, the taste.

Xavier's mind exploded into tiny fragments of desire. The taste of her was beyond what he'd ever imagined. Sweet and hot and liquid, and hungry. Fuck, so hungry. And he wanted to consume her. Fill his body with hers.

Her arms went around his neck and she moaned into his mouth. The sound went straight to his dick, and he nipped at her, suckled her lower lip, then kissed her passionately once again. Oh Christ, this was it. She was perfect. *His* perfect. The way she moved, touched him, molded to him—wanted him. He'd never be able

157

to go back from here. He'd felt her and tasted her now. Her heat and her desire belonged to him. How could he ever let another soul get close to her again?

And then her hands moved down to his shoulders and his back, her nails digging into his skin as her teeth bit at his tongue, and he lost all control. All that remained in the darkness, in the shadows, were two desperate, ravenous puma shifters. Groaning her name, Xavier crushed her against him, ravaged her mouth, pressed his thigh up harder against her sex, feeling the wet heat of her pussy. He wanted inside her, belonged inside her. He wanted to take her—lift up her dress, rip off her panties and fuck her right there. He didn't care who saw them. In fact, in that moment, he wanted spectators. Wanted every last Pantera male to know who Amalie belonged to.

The thought killed him. Stopped him.

As did the look in her drowsy, sex-hazed eyes when he eased back from her.

"Shit," he whispered so close to her mouth their breath co-mingled.

She swallowed, her eyes trying to focus. "Xavier."

His name on her lips had Xavier's cock straining against the zipper of his jeans. His eyes cut left, past her ear. Hiss was still searching, irritation and concern playing about his features. "I'm so sorry, Amalie."

"Don't say that," she warned.

"Oh, fuck, this was a mistake."

"Or that."

He wanted to let her go, release her, but he couldn't make himself do it. Though Hiss hadn't seen them yet, he was drawing closer to where they hid. A low, terrifying growl erupted from Xavier's throat, and he knew that if the Hunter male got within a foot of Amalie right now, he might actually attack, maybe even kill him. He was that jacked up—that proprietary. His puma snarled and ripped at his insides, and to save himself, and possibly the Hunter male as well, he allowed it to break free.

He stumbled back, away from Amalie, and shifted into his cat.

"Xavier," she said, her voice threaded with heat.

He looked at her for one brief moment, saw her anger and hurt, and enduring lust, and let his puma snarl and hiss before turning and stalking away. From the party, the food, the music, the sexually-charged atmosphere.

And from the female he could never taste again—no matter how desperately he wanted her.

CHAPTER SIX

Furious and turned-on so badly she just wanted to go to her room and find comfort in her own hand, Mal burst into the house. Poor Hiss. He deserved an amazing female. Not some dope with a relentless crush. The Hunter male was gorgeous and honorable, and more than a few female eyes had covetously followed him around the fete tonight. He could've stayed—should've stayed—when she'd told him she wanted to go home. But he'd insisted on escorting her.

While Xavier had left her alone, panting, confused and pissed off.

Xavier.

That goddamn male had ruined her. Truly. First when she had fallen in both lust and love for him on that birthday in the bayou, and now tonight, when he'd given her a moment of that fantasy, then ripped it away. No, not just ripped it away, but ripped it into shreds.

As she slammed the door and started down the hall, the memory of his hands on her, his mouth on her, mingled with his apologies and regrets. Fuck him, she didn't want it—neither one. Why couldn't he get that? She wasn't asking for a future or a promise or a mating. All she wanted was him.

For him to be her first.

The sound of running water curbed her emotional and frustrated thoughts momentarily, and instead of heading for her room, she turned down the hall toward the door that led to the outside shower. She knew who was out there, *in* there. With every step, every shaky breath, her hand curling around the door handle, she warned herself to stop and walk away. *Go into your room, take care of yourself and go to sleep.*

But like the cat she was, her hunger for prey— shit, for the prey of a lifetime—could not be quelled. For better or for worse, Xavier was her fantasy, her addiction, and he was in there, nude, wet, steam rising off his thickly muscled body. She had to see it. See him.

Without another thought, she pulled off her dress, panties and bra, and tossed them to the ground.

***

His hand wrapped around his cock, Xavier leaned against the rock wall, hot water pummeling his shoulders and back. He was such a fuck. Touching her, tasting her. He had no self-control and no honor. And he couldn't blame it on the fete or the moon or the purple lilies. That stunning need, that irrepressible want, it still ran through him like a vindictive snake in his blood.

Groaning, growling, he pumped himself from root to tip, trying like hell to see a blank screen on the lids of his eyes. But it was no use. She was there now. Imprinted. In that dress and out of it. Smiling at him, laughing, biting his lip as her nails dug into the skin of his back.

Come leaked from the tip of his dick and he ran his fingers over the head. But as he slid his palm back up his shaft, a warm hand suddenly closed around his and squeezed.

"Releasing some tension?" a female voice whispered seductively.

Xavier's head jacked up, his eyes slammed open and he released his hold on his cock. "What the hell, Amalie—"

She wrapped her hand around his shaft again and uttered, "Don't move." Then looked up at him with accusing eyes. "You kissed me tonight."

Her hand, hot and soft, held him with such possessive skill. He groaned, "Oh, fuck."

"That's not an answer, an explanation or an apology." Wearing nothing but a fierce, highly sexual smile, she tightened her grip on his cock.

Christ, he wanted to move, wanted to thrust into her hot, little palm. "It was a mistake, Amalie," he ground out, his heart slamming against his ribs.

"Maybe." She snarled softly. "Probably. But it happened, and I can't forget it. Can you?"

His cock turned to steel in her hand.

Feeling what she did to him—what just her words did to him—she grinned and started to stroke him. "I didn't think so."

Cursing inwardly, Xavier stared at her, his nostrils flaring with each breath he dragged into his lungs. Steam raged around them, but it did nothing to mask her nude body. Her insanely hot nude body.

He'd imagined, fantasized about what she'd look like under her clothes, standing before him, stretched out on his bed, her arms above her head. But it was nothing to the reality. She was perfection. Her legs were long and tight with muscle, her small waist flared upward to strong, toned arms and luscious shoulders. But it was her chest, her large, heavy breasts that made his mouth water and his hands fist in anticipation.

"Why did you come home early, Amalie?" he said hoarsely, his gaze flipping up to meet hers.

Beautiful dark green eyes flared with emerald heat. "I got tired of playing games. Pretending. It wasn't fair to Hiss."

"Hiss." His eyes narrowed. "Did the Hunter male touch you?"

Her tongue darted out to swipe at her bottom lip. "The only one who touched me tonight was you, Xavier." She reached down with her other hand and cupped his heavy sack, rolled his balls between her fingers. "And it wasn't enough. In fact, it was a goddamn tease."

The muscles in his abdomen tensed and he groaned. "Fuck...You're going to make me come."

"Good." She drew closer to him, under the hot spray, her strokes to his shaft growing faster, tighter. "Tell me."

"What?" His body flexed in anticipation of climax, and he had to do everything in his power not to grab her hips and ram her up against the stone wall, fuck her blind—fuck her blissful.

"Tell me why you didn't want me with him," she said, her words a whispered demand.

He pinned her with a predatory stare and growled out, "I don't want you with anyone."

She leaned even closer, pumping him off as she brushed her pebbled nipples against his chest. "Why? Tell me why."

"No one's good enough for you, Amalie," he rasped, his cock growing harder, thicker.

"Not even you?"

He cursed and thrust himself into her fist. "Especially not me."

"That's bullshit," she said before dipping her head to his chest. "And you know it. Christ, you'd better know it."

She didn't say another word. Her mouth closed around his nipple, and as she stroked him, played with him, she sucked and scraped her teeth across his flesh.

Xavier was lost to what he knew to be right and wrong. What he believed she deserved. She had taken him over. She owned him. And there was no going back. He bucked, ground his hips, pistoning his cock into her soft, wicked hand as she stroked him fast. His balls tightened, filled with come, and he growled her name. His hips jerked, and hot seed burst from the head of his dick. As he came all over her hands and belly, she bit down lightly on his nipple, causing him to groan and curse, and utter her name. Over and over.

It took him only seconds to come awake, even with climax still shuddering through him. Hunger and need like he'd never known assaulted his mind and he had to have her or he was going to lose it. Snarling, his puma just millimeters below his skin, Xavier wrapped his hands around her waist and lifted her up, set her back against the shower wall, safe from the heavy spray.

"You just unlocked the puma's cage, Amalie," he said, his eyes pinned on her, his voice a dangerous, deep purr. "And he's hungry."

***

Mal felt a delicious unease move through her as Xavier lowered to one knee before her. She might be a virgin, but she was no innocent. She was Pantera, and the ways of mating were not hidden behind a curtain of immoral shame. They were offered as a way to connect, to love, to allow the puma a chance to feel human touch, and the human self a way to react with animal-like hunger. More than once, she'd come across couples in the forest, kissing, touching, even fucking, as she'd been on patrol. Normally, she'd left them to it, darted off in the opposite direction. But there had been a few times she'd stopped to watch. Hidden behind a tree, her heart pounding, her sex growing tight and wet as she observed what she'd wanted so badly.

What she'd saved for the male on his knees before her.

Xavier's ice-blue eyes drifted up her belly, to her ribs and breasts. He watched as her nipples beaded, as her chest rose and fell quickly with her excited breathing. She knew what he intended to do to her, where his mouth would go—his tongue—and as his hands wrapped around her ankles and raked upward, she moaned with anticipation.

Steam continued to rise and coil around them, protecting the moment. Xavier's eyes connected with hers then and she felt that hungry, fierce stare deep inside her sex. The greedy, eager muscles clenched, and her thighs trembled. She had to fist her hands to keep them from grabbing the back of his head and slamming his face into her pussy.

"So beautiful," he rumbled, looking at her. "Beautiful, beautiful Amalie."

Her heart squeezed with his words. He had no idea, no clue how long she'd waited to hear him talk to her that way. With both tenderness and sexual desire. It ripped her open, left her vulnerable, and she whimpered.

"Shh," he whispered, his hands lightly grazing her inner thighs as he trailed upward to her sex. When he reached her mound, he gently spread her lips wide and released a sensual groan. "Beautiful Amalie has a beautiful cunt."

It was as if Mal lost all brain function after that. As he dipped his head, ran his tongue from her opening up to her clit, she became one trembling, bundle of nerves. The feeling was too good, too overwhelmingly perfect to contain. Bracing her hands on either side of the shower walls, she watched him, his dark head between her thighs, his tongue lightly flicking over her clit. Groans escaped him, and he eased one finger inside her.

She gasped with instant pleasure. Her body had only ever known the thrust of her own fingers, and while that had felt good, this—Xavier's thick digit deep inside of her—was a thousand times better.

"Oh, Amalie," he growled against her swollen bud. "You are so tight. So hot. You wrap around me. Your sweet, honeyed walls tremble around me."

Mal's eyes closed and she let her head fall back against the stone, let the steam envelop her.

"That's right," Xavier said, easing a second finger inside her and pumping her gently. "Let me make you feel good, Amalie. Let me make you come so hard you scream. God, there's nothing I want more than to please you."

His mouth found her sex once again, and as he fingered her, deeper and deeper with each thrust, he suckled her clit, drawing on it, sending her to the purple moon and back. Her fingernails dug into the rock walls, and she whimpered and bucked against his hungry mouth as her arousal made his sexy jaw glisten.

Just when she thought she was going to explode, Xavier drew back and gentled his touch. His tongue swirled around her swollen, sensitive bud, flicking it back and forth until she gulped in air. But it was his purr that did her in, made her still, made her moan into the hot, steamy air. The vibration curled up from the back of his throat and hit his tongue.

The tongue that was pressed lightly against her clit.

With a pained, delicious cry, she fell apart under his mouth, her knees buckling, her thighs shaking. Pulling his fingers from her drenched sex, Xavier grabbed her ass, held her up as he kissed her shaking mound and licked her cream.

It seemed like hours before she came down, before her legs stopped trembling, before he stopped pleasuring her and rested his head on her abdomen.

"Xavier," she mumbled incoherently. "Take me to bed."

For several seconds, he remained silent. Then he released her and stood up. The pained and guilty expression on his gorgeous face combined with the wetness around his mouth, made her growl.

She wanted to lick him. Taste herself on him.

And then he cursed and shook his head, and ruined it for the both of them.

"Goddamn you." Her heart lurched. "You want me. I know you do."

"That's not the point," he ground out.

Her gaze searched his. "Do you think this was a mistake?"

"Oh, Amalie."

"Do you?" she demanded, feeling suddenly naked and cold and vulnerable.

"It shouldn't have happened." He looked away, his jaw as tight as the rest of him. "Fuck me."

"Yes. Fuck you."

Enough. This had to be it. This had to kill her goddamn crush once and for all, right?

Wrong, her heart whispered as it clenched miserably.

She pushed past him, stumbled out of the shower and into the fragrant night air. Tears blurred her vision as she rushed into the house and headed down the hall. What an idiot. What a stupid, foolish female. Maybe he was right. Maybe she was still a cub. Because only a cub would harbor a crush for so damned long. Only a cub would react this way: hurt and miserable, yet desperate for more. A grown female would take her orgasm and walk away satisfied.

She slammed the door to her bedroom, and headed for her bed. She was cold and wet beneath her covers, due to the fact that she hadn't dried off. But she didn't care. She just wanted to cry in peace.

She didn't hear the door open, didn't hear Xavier pad across the floor. She only sensed him, scented him, when the mattress dipped with his weight, and he curled up behind her.

"Don't ever say *fuck you* to me," he whispered into the curve of her ear.

She swallowed a sob. "Why not? You deserve it."

"Maybe, but it hurts me. Cuts me deep, Beautiful."

Swiping the tears from her eyes, she growled and rolled around to face him, connect with those killer blue eyes. "How can you say that? When it's you who's hurting me. Every time you reject me. Every time you say this is a mistake—that *we're* a mistake."

"I have to say that," he ground out, his eyes flaring with sudden and passionate heat. "Shit, Amalie." He reached out and brushed her hair off her cheek, then kept his palm there. "If I take you to bed, if I mate you, I'll claim you. Do you understand me?"

Her insides tensed. *Claimed.* She stared at him.

His eyes bore into hers, and he growled. "You'll be mine, goddamit."

"I want to be yours," she said, shaking her head. "Tonight, tomorrow, for the next three days—"

169

"No, Amalie," he cut her off, his tone deadly serious. "You'll be mine for a lifetime."

His words silenced her, made her chest ache and her mind race with thoughts, memories and wishes. She wasn't sure how to feel. She didn't want him to fuck her and stick around out of obligation. And wasn't that what he was saying? That if he slept with her, he'd feel obligated to claim her?

"Xavier, I'm not asking for anything more than this," she began. "Three days of this. I'm not asking for a commitment, a mating—"

He cut her off again, but this time with a deep, hungry kiss. It was so intense and toe-curling, Mal couldn't stop herself from moaning and snuggling in closer and wrapping her arms around his neck.

When he broke the kiss, his breathing labored and his eyes dilated, her body and her puma purred.

"This isn't about you asking, Amalie," he said with animal-like ferocity. "This isn't even about what you want—though fuck, I want to give you everything. It's about me. My regret in all of this is that because I've given in to what I want, what I'm hungry for, I don't think I can ever let you go. And if I fuck you, if our bodies connect, you will not be able to walk away from me. I won't allow it. You'll be mine. Forever. Always. No one will look at you without me growling at them. No one will touch you without getting their paws ripped off." He reached around her, grabbed her ass and hauled her tight against him. "Even now, with your cream on my tongue, down my throat, inside of me, I don't know if I can let you go."

Staring at him, her mouth open, Mal felt as though both her head and her heart might explode. "Xavier…"

"No, no," he uttered hoarsely, his hands raking up her ass to stroke her lower back. "Not tonight, Beautiful. No more tonight. Just let me hold you while you sleep. Let me feel your warmth, your skin against mine."

CHAPTER SEVEN

Light shocked the backs of Xavier's eyes as he came awake. He could count on one hand the number of times he'd slept all night—been able to sleep all night. Normally, his mind was so thick with ideas, moving too rapidly as he built codes and cracked codes, that he couldn't calm himself enough to sleep well.

But last night had been different.

He growled softly, reveling in the heat and sweet scent of the female curled up into him, her back against his chest and groin. Nothing had prepared him for the depth of desire he'd experienced on his knees before her in the shower. The surge of possessiveness. Even as he held her now, even as his cock filled with blood and grew hard against his belly, he felt it.

Mine.

The haze of sleep still within him, Xavier lowered his head and kissed the back of her neck. She had the most beautiful skin, softness over lean muscle. He was about to follow the line of her backbone with his mouth, all the way down to the curve of her sweet ass, and into heaven once again, when his smartphone rang out from the living room. He wanted to ignore it. He even lifted his hand toward the door and flipped it off,

172

but he knew it could be news about the camera's owner, perhaps even news about Chayton. They were counting on him—Raphael, Ashe, the elders, the Pantera—he'd given his word.

With a quick kiss to her shoulder, promising himself he'd be back beneath the sheets before she even woke up, Xavier left the warmth of her bed and padded out into the hallway.

He swiped the phone from the top of the couch, pressed the answer button and muttered in an irritated voice, "Yeah."

"Shit, X." Captain's laughter rang out on the other end. "Wrong side of the bed?"

Right side. Perfect side. "What's going on, Cap?"

"I have something for you. Got your computer open?"

Rounding the couch, Xavier had both computers open, and his cell on speaker before he even sat down. "Go."

"Tracked down the store that sold the camera," Captain said, his voice booming through the speaker Xavier had attached to one of the computers.

Xavier could hear the male working the keyboard hard and fast. "With the serial number?"

"Yep."

"Show me."

Instantly, both the camera shop website and a copy of the receipt popped up on his screen. Xavier enhanced it while Captain explained, "This place stores their records digitally, which is a space saver, but there was a weakness in their backup files I used my genius to exploit."

Xavier snorted at the male's smugness. "No address?" he asked, his fingers moving over the keyboard a mile a minute.

"Whoever bought it paid in cash and in person."

"Fuck me."

"No, no, bro. Here's the part you're going to love." His puma grin was practically audible. "Maybe it'll even pull you out of the shit-tastic mood you're in."

"Doubt it." He forced his mind to focus. Not on the bed and the warm, wet naked female within it, but on his work.

"Our camera owner emailed the store," Captain told him proudly.

"No shit."

"A service problem. Seems the camera's battery life wasn't as long as promised."

This was good. Damned good. He'd been hoping, but so far the leads had gone dead. Could their target have actually left a digital fingerprint for them? "You trace it?"

"Yeah. No luck yet. The trail keeps bouncing all over the globe. Whoever we're dealing with has definitely got an encrypted router on his PC—or whatever computer he or she is using."

Xavier grinned as the email address popped up on his screen. "Could we possibly be dealing with a techie here?"

"I don't know. But either way, this is your department now. No one cracks code like you, *mon ami*. It's fucking art."

"Thanks, brother. Soon as I get a location I'm going to check it out in person, see if this human can lead us to Chayton. I'll be on the cell if you guys need me."

Captain paused, then sniffed. "Tracking offline and on foot? Isn't that a Hunter's job?"

"Why, yes, it is," came a female voice behind him.

Xavier whirled around, growled at the intruder. The very sexy, nearly naked, intruder. She was standing in the doorway of her bedroom, wearing only a tank top that barely covered her shaved mound. Blood surged into his dick, and even though his fellow Geek couldn't see shit through his phone, Xavier felt possessive ire barrel through him.

"Gotta go, Cap," he muttered to the male. "I'll be in touch."

Xavier didn't even wait for the male to reply, just hit the off button and stood. "You should've stayed in bed."

"Why? Were you planning on coming back?"

"Hell, yes."

As her mouth curved into a wicked grin, her gaze drifted down his body, lingering on the thick erection pressing against his lower abdomen. "Too bad we have to go. Get to work."

The word *we* wasn't lost on Xavier, and he shook his head. "Not happening, Beautiful."

She leaned against the door, the action causing the edges of her tank to lift, giving him an unobstructed view of her glorious pussy.

His mouth watered. God, he wanted to taste her again. Spread her thighs and send his tongue up inside her slick, hot channel until she screamed.

But that spot in hell beside Shakpi was growing closer by the second.

"I'm one of the best trackers in the Wildlands, Xavier," she said, her eyes searching his now.

"I'm going outside of the Wildlands, Amalie," he countered.

Her kitty cat grin widened. "Perfect. We could use a break."

"From the Pantera or from each other?"

"I'll leave that answer to you." She crossed her arms, grabbed the edges of her tank and pulled it over her head. Naked, her nipples hardening, her eyes still pinned to him, she tossed the white strip of fabric at him. "You could always leave me here. Alone." She laughed softly. "Or not."

Come leaked from the head of his dick, and a growl escaped his throat. "You play dirty."

"Oh, Xavier," she purred, "you have no idea."

She would be the death of him. Or maybe the life. He wasn't sure which option worried him more. But either way, it wasn't going to get examined in that moment. He was too worked up, and she was too tempting.

"Fine," he ground out. "Put on some goddamn clothes before I fuck you against that door."

"Promises, promises," she called as she turned around and strode back into her room.

***

Her arms wrapped around Xavier's waist, she reveled in the feel of his back against her chest and the motorcycle's engine between her legs. It wasn't as hot as riding on his puma, but it was pretty damn close.

Getting dressed and leaving the house, and the Wildlands, had taken supreme effort on both of their parts. But the reminder of why they needed to go on this mission, search out any clues to Chayton's whereabouts—find the human male before their enemies did—had sobered their desire.

The heat of the day grew thicker as they drew closer to Lafayette. Insects hit the plastic visors of their helmets, and Mal wished she'd worn something lighter than a black leather jacket over her blue tank. Xavier's friend had tracked the IP address to two possible locations. A coffee shop in Lafayette and a cabin in the swamps. They'd gone to the coffee shop first. The owner had been friendly enough, but hadn't given them anything major to go on. Seemed folks with laptops were in and out of the shop all day long. The human male explained that he recognized some of them, didn't know others, but he rarely got intimate enough with anyone to glean personal information.

Now, as the day started to wane into late afternoon, they were headed for the cabin.

"Wrap your arms tighter around me, Amalie," Xavier called back to her as he took a curve with practiced skill.

"I'm not going to fall off," she shouted.

"Who said anything about you falling off?" He took one hand off the bars and used it to press her arms closer. "I just like the feel of you."

She grinned and rubbed her chin against his shoulder. Fantasy or reality. For three days or one. It just didn't matter. She'd never felt so happy. "I won't forget you said that," she called to him.

He growled back, "Good."

After another stretch of curves, one hill and a bumpy-ass bridge, Xavier finally slowed and pulled onto a road marked, '*Swamp Estates. Private Property.*' As they kicked up crazy amounts of dust on the dirt pathway, Amalie couldn't help laughing.

"What's so funny?" Xavier asked as they entered a small parking lot and slid into one of many empty spots.

"*Estates* is really pushing things," she said as he killed the engine and got off the bike. "*Rustic cabins* is way more like it."

Xavier glanced over his shoulder at the ten or so cabins dotting the swamp's lip in the distance. "Never underestimate the subliminal powers of marketing, Beautiful." He turned back to face her, his eyes flashing. "Sometimes to accept what we're given in this life, to be content with it, we have to amplify or change its value."

Good god, was it possible that she loved this male even more for his incredible brain than his knee-weakening body? She studied him. And tried to pretend she hadn't just used the word 'love' in her mental query regarding how she felt about him.

"Have you ever done that?" she asked. "Changed the value of something you had to accept?"

"Sure."

Her heart stuttered. "When?"

He didn't answer right away, seemed to be mulling something over in his head. Then he glanced past her to the road they'd just traveled, and scrubbed a hand over his face. "When my father died."

It was something she'd known about, had heard about, but they hadn't been close enough to talk about back then. She hoped they were now. Or getting there. She fought the urge to reach for his hand. She didn't want to do anything to stop him from opening up to her, being vulnerable. "How did you amplify that? Or change its value?"

With a tight exhale, his gaze slid back to meet hers. "I got to have two families."

It took her all of five seconds to glean his meaning, but it made her gut ache. His family was Aristide, maybe even her. And he'd crossed a line he hadn't wanted to cross. "I understand."

"Do you?" he asked, his eyes now piercing in the light of the late afternoon sun. "Because I really need you to."

Before Mal could answer, the rumbling sounds of a car coming up the dirt path rent the air. It was coming fast toward them, into the parking lot, kicking up a shitload of dust. Her Hunter instincts kicking into high gear, Mal grabbed Xavier's hand, and took off for the shelter of the trees down near the swamp.

Silently, they watched the car slide into a parking space and stop with a sputter and a groan. When the door opened and a woman got out, Mal turned to Xavier and whispered, "She look familiar? From any of the shop pictures on the drive?"

He shook his head.

She pressed him. "You sure? There had to have been a ton of film."

He turned and gave her a lopsided grin. "I have a photographic memory, Beautiful."

Her heart freaking swooned, and she uttered dryly, "Of course you do."

He laughed softly. "It's a damn inconvenience. Every inch of your body…" He tapped his temple. "All up here and never going away."

"Good." It was her turn to grin now.

He motioned for her to follow. "Come."

"You have the cabin number, right?"

"I think so," he said, following the water, keeping to the shadows, the shade. "If I can remember it."

She gave him a playful push, laughing softly. At which he growled, and yanked her to his side. But as they drew closer to the cabins, they quieted, moving swiftly, listening, eyes wary as they passed the rustic dwellings, their screened porches overlooking the cypress swamp, now tinted peach in the light of the late-afternoon sun.

"Are we breaking and entering?" she asked, wiping sweat from her brow. "Or just lying in wait to grab the guy?"

He turned his gaze on her. "That's the Hunters way, isn't it, Amalie? No talk, all action."

"Not this Hunter," she said in a hushed voice as they approached the rear of the cabin. "I like talk. Lots of it. In my ear is good. Against my mouth even better."

With a soft snarl, he whirled around and caught her up in his arms. His ice blue eyes narrowed with heat. "Don't make me regret bringing you."

"Oh, you won't." With a crooked smile, she pulled away from him. "I have the nose after all."

"The nose, the eyes, the mouth, the ass…"

She glanced back and winked at him, then darted away, quick and quiet, to the side door of the cabin. She was there only a few seconds, when Xavier came up behind her, whispered in her ear, "Well?"

She shivered. In the ninety-plus degree weather, she actually shivered. "No one's in there."

"No body heat."

She glanced over her shoulder and grinned. "No body heat and no heartbeat. Should we wait inside?"

He shook his head. "Maybe in another cabin close by. Maybe in the trees."

She looked up at the massive cypress overhead. "If only I could access my puma," she whispered. "I hate that we can't shift outside the Wildlands. It's so inconvenient." Then her eyes slid down to meet his and she added, "And that pussy of mine really knows how to dig in her nails and climb."

Her suggestive tone and words had Xavier's nostrils flaring, and he took her hand and led her away from the cabin and back toward the swamp. "I think we'll stay out of the trees for today," he grumbled. "Come, Female."

CHAPTER EIGHT

"Liar!"

"Excuse me?" Xavier didn't spare her a glance, though he wanted to. Shit, he always wanted to. After all, she looked hot. Jeans, tank, smooth, tanned skin with a light sheen of sweat. His tongue twitched inside his mouth at the image, at the yearning to taste her salty skin. But he had to set his position, make sure he could see if and when someone returned to that cabin.

"You said no trees, and look at this," she said behind him.

Crouched inside the shelter of a massive fallen cypress, Xavier shrugged. "No climbing was needed." He narrowed his eyes at the screened porch a couple hundred yards away. "We're protected here. We can see everything, and no one can see us."

"We could be protected inside one of those cabins bracketing our camera owner."

Xavier glanced over his shoulder. Damn, she looked beautiful. Edible. "You looking for some comfort on this mission, Hunter?" he asked.

Her lips twitched. "No," she returned haughtily, the leaves of the cypress overhead traveling back and forth across her back. "I'm just saying there are options…"

"Like carpet and walls and indoor plumbing?"

She shook her head. "You're such a guy."

"Damn right," he said, then growled softly. "Wait, what does that mean?"

She laughed. "With what you have between your legs, you don't need indoor plumbing. Us females…well, let's just say it's an awkward act without it. Out of our fur, at any rate. "

He laughed with her. "I can ask if there are any vacancies here. Hell, maybe I'll just kick out some nice couple celebrating their mating night if it would please you."

She sobered suddenly, and her expression went soft, sensual. Even her tone was far more tantalizing than teasing. "You want to please me?"

Christ, she made him insane. His hands curled into fists, and a low, husky growl exited his throat. "Don't act so surprised, Hunter. I may be a closed book when it comes to sharing feelings and all that sappy bullshit, but don't pretend you don't know how affected I am by you. How my body twitches and hardens and sweats every fucking moment you're around. Pleasing you?" He laughed darkly. "It's on my mind constantly."

Her breathing quickened, making her cheeks flush and her spectacular chest rise and fall.

"Well, you're not the only one," she said, her eyes pinned to his.

"What do you mean?"

A slow, sexy grin played about her lips. "Pleasing me is on my mind constantly, too."

"You!" With a fierce growl, Xavier forgot everything—where he was, why he was there—and leapt on top of her, forcing her to her back on the soft moss. Snarling down at her, he rasped, "You…Dammit…You…"

She gazed up at him, breathing so hard, she could hardly get the word, "What?" out of her mouth.

"You make me crazy," he growled.

She raked her hands up his chest. "Good."

"You make me hungry," he continued, his eyes narrowed slits as he ground his hips, his hard cock, against her sex.

"Finally," she uttered, grinning, her hands moving down, over his stomach toward his hips.

He groaned, knowing where she was headed. "You make me…God, Amalie…"

"What, Xavier? Tell me. Please, tell me."

"You make me so fucking happy."

The words were out of his mouth before he could take them back. Not that he wanted to. They were true. He'd never felt anything close to this with anyone. He wanted her. Not just a night—or three—of hot, mindless fucking. No. He *wanted* her.

Amalie's hands froze near his hipbones and her eyes searched his. Within their incredible green depths, he saw her heart. Saw how she felt about him. How she'd always felt about him. And if he wasn't mistaken, he saw his own heart reflected there, too.

Suddenly, her face broke with a grin, and she whispered, "By the way, I don't think anyone would be having their mating night here."

"Why not?" he asked, his hands cupping her face. Her soft, beautiful face.

"It's just not very romantic. The swamp, the bugs."

He ran his thumb across her lower lip. "You sure you're a Hunter, Amalie?"

Her soft, sexy laughter went straight to his dick. "All I'm saying is that when you mate, or marry as the humans say, you want that first night to be special."

His expression grew serious and he leaned down and kissed her lower lip. "No bugs?" he whispered.

She nodded, lifting her chin instinctively. "Preferably."

He kissed her top lip, then swiped it gently with his tongue. "No swamp?"

"If one can help it," she said breathlessly, her arms wrapping around his waist.

Heat surged up from her skin into his and he stifled a groan. "What if one can't help it?"

Her eyes cut to his mouth and she licked her lips. "Xavier…"

"Because I don't think I can help it. I don't think I want to, Hunter."

She smiled softly, sweetly. "That's '*Beautiful*' to you."

"Yes, it is." He kissed her, a kiss that conveyed his hunger and his need, but there was so much more. More he had to say. The one vital thing that would change everything between them. He pulled back and forced her gaze to lock with his. "I want you, Amalie."

She arched her back and purred, "Then have me."

His cock felt so hard it was painful. "It's your first mating."

"I know," she thrust her hips up, ground her sex against him brazenly. "I want it to be with you. I've always wanted it to be with you."

Pain and pleasure battled within him. "I want that too. Fuck…"

"Then take it," she said harshly, desperately.

"Here? Now?"

"Do you care where we are?" she demanded. "Do you care who sees us right now?" She cursed. "Do you care if everything is put on hold for however long we need? However long it takes for this to happen between us?"

"Fuck no. Fuck. No." His mouth was so dry. He needed her, her heat, her saliva, her cream. He didn't give a shit about where they were, but he needed her to understand something. He needed her to know what he was asking of her. "Amalie, I won't take it unless I can keep it."

Her eyes widened, a flash of confusion moving through them. "What do you mean?"

"You know what I mean." He rose up, his eyes pinned to hers, but his fingers moving to the waistband of her jeans. "I want you. But not for a night or three." He flicked the button, eased down the zipper. "I want you always, forever, until the Wildlands are no longer filled with magic and we are dust that a new species calls their home."

For a moment, all Xavier heard was her rapid breathing and the sounds of the water and the wind through the cypress.

"I love you, Amalie," he said in a hoarse, desperate voice. "Fuck, Beautiful, I always have. I don't care about anything or anyone. Not anymore—not ever."

Tears sprang to her eyes, turning them a shocking leaf green in the light of fading sun.

"I love you, too," she uttered. "But you know that. You've always known."

He nodded. "Tell me," he nearly begged. "Tell me before I die of longing. Tell me before I strip you bare and taste you, fuck you, claim you. Tell me I'm yours and you're mine."

"Are you sure?" she said as he pulled down her underwear and jeans and tossed them aside. "Forever is—"

"What I want more than anything in the world, Beautiful," he said, easing her tank over her head and her bra from her shoulders. "There's nothing, no one, who can stop this, can stop me from claiming you." His eyes flipped up to lock on hers. "Except you."

Shock barreled through Xavier as Amalie grasped both sides of his T-shirt and ripped it up the center. The sounded echoed across the bayou, but he barely heard it. Her words next drowned out everything else.

"Mate me, Xavier," she said, her eyes flashing. "Mate me for life."

She had the black fabric off his body in seconds and was working his jeans down his hips before he had time to register her movement. Once he did though, he was like a male possessed, growling, taking over, his jeans off and discarded, and his head between her thighs.

The liquid heat that hit his tongue made come leak from his cock. She tasted like heaven, like honey, and he licked her over and over, nothing gentle, nothing sweet. Fuck no. Right now, he just wanted to eat her. And if the way her hips were jacking up, pumping hungrily against his mouth, was any indicator, she liked his slight roughness, his need to consume her.

"Oh god, Xavier," she said on a moan. "I can't...it's too much."

Damn right. It was all too much. But so what? They both needed this, needed each other. More was good. More made her buck and groan. More made her pussy so wet and warm and soft, he couldn't wait to get inside her.

Her fingers plunged into his hair, her nails digging into his scalp as he tongued her deep, then pulled out and suckled her clit.

"You're making me crazy," she whispered, then gasped as he pressed his tongue against her and jerked his head up and down.

Xavier felt her violent shudder beneath his mouth, coming hard and intense against his tongue. His entire body went up in flames as her juices rushed him. He lapped at her, drank her up, but left enough wet heat to coat her pussy walls and make his thrust easy and pleasurable.

With one last possessive suckle to her swollen clit, he rose over her, catching his weight on his elbows, holding his position so they were face to face. Breathing heavily, her eyes filled with heat and deep desire, Amalie wrapped her legs around his waist, arched her back and brazenly and seductively licked him from chin to nose.

"Mmm," she uttered, her eyes lifting to his. "I taste good on you."

Xavier, the male, died.

While the animal within him flared to the surface of his skin and took hold, took control. His cock poised at her entrance, the head hard and wet with pre-come, he growled. "Mine."

She nodded. "Yours."

And he pushed inside her.

***

He was deep.

Breathstealingly deep.

Every thick, hard inch, was deliciously impaled inside her, all the way to her womb, and nothing—*nothing*—had ever felt so amazing. There was no pain, just a wondrous full feeling. God, they were truly made for each other. She'd known the first time she'd seen him. Too young to understand the bond, the connection, it had surfaced as a lust and a hope for the future.

But now, now as he started moving inside of her, claiming her with his body as he looked down into her eyes, connected with her, she understood the true symmetry of love. Him and Her. Even in their puma forms, they would know this bond, feel this bond.

"I love this," he rasped, nipping at her lips as he thrust gently inside of her, getting her body ready for the intense, possessive thrusts to come.

After all, he was a Pantera male. They could fuck gently, of course. But it was only a matter of time before they went wild, attacked, demanded, their animal nature ruling their sex drive.

And being a Pantera female, Mal couldn't wait.

"I love being inside of you," he continued, dropping his head, taking one hard nipple into his mouth and suckling it deep. To her gasp, the rush of wet heat inside her pussy, he growled. "Kissing you, sucking your sweet, pink tits. Feeling you go tight and hot around my cock whenever I do."

His words, uttered against her breast, his breath teasing her wet nipple, made Mal feel like she was going to come again. She fought against it. She wanted to come with him this second time.

Then he look up and smiled. "And shit, Beautiful, I just love you."

Mal didn't know if it was the words, his voice, or how his ice blue eyes had melted into lazy, erotic pools of emotional blue, but she couldn't stop herself. Her Hunter strength kicked in, and she pressed her hands to his hips, eased his cock out of her, and flipped to her belly.

"Fuck me now," she demanded, coming up on her hands and knees. "Fuck me hard and deep until we both come. Outside, under the sky, near the bayou. This is how you should claim me, and how I should be taken. My pussy—both the one who purrs for you, and the one you're looking at right now—need it."

Xavier didn't say a word. Maybe he couldn't. Maybe his animal was right there, hissing and snapping and snarling near the surface of his skin, just as hers was. But it was no more than a second before she felt him behind her, his thick, stone-hard cock pressed at her entrance.

His thrust wasn't gentle this time.

Thank. Fucking. Christ.

He knew what she wanted, and he was giving it to her. Gripping her hips, he rode her hard, working her so deep she moaned and keened and circled her hips trying to feel him from every angle. Shock waves of pleasure moved through her. How could something so primal feel so good? So beyond amazing. She wanted to cry and scream and laugh and warn him to never stop. That as mates she would demand he fuck her every day and every night for the rest of her life. But she didn't have the voice. He'd stripped her bare in too many ways to count.

And then she felt it. The thing—the amazing, magical thing she'd only heard about from her Pantera female friends. The sign of a true mating. She felt his claws against the skin of her hip, and as he pounded into her, and she stretched around him, he marked her. She cried out, from pain, from pleasure, and from the absolute wonder of having a long-realized dream come true.

"I love you, Amalie," he said on a fierce growl.

He drove up into her, so deep she gasped, then reached around to palm her drenched pussy. With one pinch to her clit, Mal came, spasming around his cock as her body went wild and uncontrolled, and a rush of hot seed filled her sex.

CHAPTER NINE

Coming down from the fuck of the century wasn't easy or fast.

Xavier was shaking. Christ, shaking. And his dick was still hard. Nothing had or would ever compare to this. Mating Amalie. She was his everything now. His life, his breath, his vision, and his reason for waking up and...god help him, hitting the sheets every night. Looking at her, sitting before her, gloriously nude, her skin sweaty and pink, his mark on her hip, her sex still glistening with their shared climaxes, he wanted her again.

And again.

Shit, he didn't even want to take her back to the Wildlands, let other males see her. He knew that was an irrational thought, and he wasn't about to share it. But it was there. Oh yeah, it was there.

But he'd sensed something, his Pantera instincts overriding his post-orgasmic shakes. A male. Human. Near the bayou.

Xavier's narrowed gaze searched the green, the trees, the calm surface of the water.

"I scent him, too," Amalie said, the vigilant Hunter back in her eyes. She grabbed her clothes and yanked them on. "Maybe it's just another guest, but we need to be ready if it's not."

Xavier had his clothes on in under ten seconds, his eyes back on the cabin. "I don't see him. I don't see anyone."

"Bayou," Amalie whispered.

Xavier turned back toward the swamp. "What the hell?"

A heavy mist now coated the surface of the bayou. A low hanging cloud moving toward them. It swirled, and seemed to have an eye in the center like a tornado. Xavier slipped in front of Amalie, closer to the four foot tall and ten foot wide mass of white haze. He didn't know what was coming, but it wouldn't get near his mate.

As it touched down at the shore, and a male emerged from that 'eye' Amalie gasped under her breath, "Holy shit."

Still hidden from view within the massive tree, Xavier stared, riveted, ready to pounce. This was a human walking past them only ten or so feet away, but clearly he was so much more than that. And when the man drew closer to the cabin, and his hand reached for the screen door, Xavier knew in his gut, they not only had their camera owner, but they might very well have The Shaman, Chayton as well.

Clearly thinking the same thing, Amalie pushed past him and ran toward the cabin and the male. Cursing, Xavier burst out of the shelter of the tree and went after her. He reached her just as she cornered the male inside his screened-in porch.

"Who are you?" she demanded.

Xavier drew closer to his mate's side. "I believe this is the human we seek, Amalie." He eyed the confused and fearful older male. "Chayton, I presume?"

***

"Isi is in the Wildlands?" he repeated, shocked and amazed. "Oh, thank the gods."

Seated across from Chayton, who had only a short time ago emerged from the bayou like a spirit, Mal nodded. "You didn't know?"

He shook his head, his nearly black eyes softening. "I couldn't find her. I've been so worried—"

"Because she wasn't in her shop?" Mal finished. "Visible on the camera you hid?"

He looked at her for a moment, his eyes searching hers. Then he nodded, "That's right. I wanted to know she was safe, even if it wasn't safe for me to watch over her in person. She is my daughter. I love her."

"Then come back to the Wildlands and see her," Mal said quickly.

It was as if an icy wind blasted through the porch. Chayton shook his head. "Impossible."

"You don't understand how vital this is," Xavier began. He was seated beside Mal, and had his hand resting protectively on her lower back. "One of the Pantera's greatest enemies is growing in power."

A different kind of heat glinted in those dark eyes. "You speak of Shakpi."

Mal's heart stuttered. "You know?"

The male pushed his long, black braid over one tanned shoulder and nodded. "Of course I know. I have come to suspect that I am the one who accidentally opened the portal."

Mal turned to Xavier, who gave her a worried look before she turned back to Chayton. "How?"

"That doesn't matter."

"Of course it does," Mal insisted harshly. "Isi is being blamed for it. The elders claim that your vision proves—"

"That damned vision," Chayton said passionately. "It has ruined so much, so many. '*The blood of The Shaman's firstborn shall carry the taint of Shakpi, releasing her powers upon the lands of the Pantera.*'" He stood and walked over to the screen that faced the bayou. With the sun's retreat, the sky was giving itself over to twilight. "It doesn't mean Isi is destined to hurt the land. The Wildlands, after all, were created by the blood of both Shakpi and Opela. The rot of the land began long before Isi's birth." He glanced over his shoulder. "If you and your kind want to blame the spread of poison, then you should point the finger at the elders who were too eager to use my powers to walk among the spirits.

Mal understood his passion, his fear. But right now, they needed his help. His daughter needed his help. "You believe it was your connection to the spirits that caused the damage?"

He sighed. "I fear that the connection unknowingly opened the portal that Shakpi is using to touch this world."

Xavier cursed, stood. "Then you have to come back and close it."

A flare of anger vibrated through Chayton, and his lean face grew tense. "No. It's too dangerous. This swamp is protected with deep magic. If I leave, they'll find me."

"Who?" both Xavier and Mal said together.

"Shakpi's followers. They'll force me to open the portal to Shakpi's prison completely."

"We won't allow them to take you," Xavier said firmly. "Come back. Let this nightmare end for us all."

He shook his head. "I'm sorry."

His resignation sent Mal into desperate mode, and she tried another tactic. "Then at least come back and see your daughters."

His face went blank. "Daughters?"

She walked over to him, put her hand on his bare arm. "Ashe is there, too, Chayton."

"What?" The word came out so softly it was a mere exhale.

"She's mated to a Pantera."

Tears pricked his dark eyes, making them glitter like polished stones. "Ashe," he uttered. "I haven't seen her since..." He shook his head, too emotional to continue.

"She's pregnant."

His eyes widened. "No."

"Yes," Xavier confirmed, moving to stand beside Mal, his hand reaching for hers. "The first cub in so many years. Our miracle."

Mal squeezed her mate's large, warm hand, but to the Shaman male, she smiled and said, "They need you, Chayton. We all need you."

CHAPTER TEN

Night blanketed the Wildlands, and though the scent of the Dyesse Lily still clung to anything with leaves or moss, the brilliant moon overhead had returned to its natural state of white. It glowed down upon them, lighting their way as they raced, in their puma state, side by side over rocks and snaking around trees, toward town. Xavier carried Chayton on his back, while Amalie, after leaving the motorcycle in its garage near the border, had been vigilant about anything or anyone following them.

As they broke through the final barrier of brush and entered town, Xavier felt the male on his back shudder. He didn't blame Chayton for his fears and concerns. With what awaited Xavier when Aristide left the confines of quarantine and learned of his and Amalie's mating, he certainly understood them. But unfaced challenges had a way of growing out of control. It was always better to deal than run.

Beside him, Amalie slowed, growling as many Pantera, both in and out of shift, came out of their dwellings to watch the arrival of The Shaman. Clearly, the text he'd sent both Raphael and Parish had gone through. He wouldn't be surprised if the elders were at the foot of the path leading to the clinic, waiting, hungry for blood and information.

But the only Pantera out in front of the clinic were Raphael, Parish and Isi's mate, Talon. All three had tight, apprehensive expressions under the stark light of the moon, and when Xavier came to a halt in front of them, he gave a quick growl of warning. Chayton had come to help, to see his daughters. Scaring him or demanding from him before he'd even set his foot on Wildlands soil was not going to happen.

Catching his puma's eye, Raphael gave Xavier a clipped nod of understanding, then turned to face Chayton. "It's good to have you here."

"I wish to see my daughters," Chayton said, climbing off Xavier's back.

"Of course," Raphael said, though his tone had a trace of warning, of protective male. "Ashe is my mate."

For a moment, Chayton didn't speak. He glanced back at Xavier, and at Amalie, who remained in her puma form, too. He gave them a tight smile, then turned back to Raphael. "I must give you my congratulations."

It was what the Suit had obviously needed to hear. His entire body relaxed and a broad grin broke on his features. "And to you," he said, then gestured toward the clinic. "Come. Both your daughters are here together."

Both, Xavier mused, watching Chayton move up the steps behind the three Pantera males. *If Isi is with Ashe, then she's out of quarantine. Which would also mean that Aristide—*

199

A growl rent the night air. It was a growl Xavier knew well. He'd heard it beside him a thousand times. His gaze flicked up. Chayton and the three Pantera males were gone. But something else far more problematic sat outside the doors to the clinic; a massive light-brown puma, black eyes flashing fire. Amalie started forward, but Xavier hissed at her to stay back. She was Aristide's sister, true, but she was also Xavier's mate, and no matter what—or who— threatened their bond, Xavier would always protect what belonged to him.

In a flash of color, Xavier shifted to male form. True to his style, Aristide shifted mid-step as he moved toward his friend. They stood at about the same height, both broad shouldered, both heavily muscled, but where Xavier was dark with light eyes, Aristide was light with dark eyes.

Beside Xavier, Amalie also shifted. And she didn't wait for either one of them to speak. "Aristide, you have no right to be pissed," she began. "You know I've been in love with this male forever. No one will make me happier. No one will love me more or protect me more fiercely or—"

"It's all right, Beautiful." Xavier stepped in front of her, and faced Aristide. This was his fight, his best friend, his betrayal. "I love her, and I've mated her."

Aristide's black eyes locked with his, and his pale brows lifted. "You've mated her?"

Xavier nodded. "There won't be an apology or a question, but there will be a promise. I'll make her happy."

200

For several long seconds, the dark-eyed male just stared at him. Then he gave a little shrug, and a broad grin split his features. "I know you will." His grin widened further. "Brother." Laughing, he grabbed Xavier and embraced him. "Shit, I've waited a long time to call you that for real."

"You asshole," Xavier muttered, clapping him on the back. "How long have you known there was something here?"

"For-freaking-ever, bro."

Xavier laughed. "Then you'll be expecting your eviction notice. She's moving out. Or you are."

"Finally. I've been waiting forever." He pushed back, turned and gave his sister a smile. "Take the house, sis. Start a new family there."

"Unbelievable," Amalie said, giving her brother a fierce glare, even when he came in for a hug. "If I'd have know this, I would've seduced Xavier a long time ago."

Aristide stiffened, and Amalie pulled away, her turn to laugh. She gave him a little wave. "Night-night, *bro.*"

As she walked away, she heard her brother growl at Xavier. "Wait? What did she just say? She seduced you?"

"Damn right. Best thing that ever happened to me," Xavier said with a grin in his voice. "Later, A."

Amalie was barely down the path when Xavier came up behind her and scooped her up in his arms. She let out a squeal of delight.

"Where are you taking me, mate of mine?" she asked, grinning up at him.

His smile was wide and hungry, and his eyes glowed blue fire in the moonlight. "Home, Beautiful."

"Mine or yours?"

He leaned in and kissed her, growled against her lips. "There is no mine or yours anymore. Only ours. So says the mark on your sexy hip."

Her skin tingled with his words, and her heart squeezed. She'd hoped and wished for this for so long, and now he was finally hers. The love of her life.

"You don't have to rush, Xavier," she giggled as he stalked through town toward their house. "We have so much longer than three days. We have forever. We have a lifetime."

But he didn't slow. In fact, he quickened his pace. "I need you now, Beautiful," he rasped. "I need to carry you home and get you in our bed. I need to strip you bare and lick every inch of your skin." He growled. "That quickie in the swamp only wet my appetite."

Her entire body flared with heat. "That was a quickie?" she nearly choked out.

He chuckled, low and sexy. "Oh, yeah."

She sighed and snuggled deeper into his chest as he rushed through the gate of their house, their home. "Oh, I have so much to learn, Xavier."

"And I can't wait to teach you, Beautiful." With a fierce snarl, he kicked down the door. "Don't worry, I'll fix that later."

"Much later," she teased.

"Tomorrow," he rasped, stalking down the hall.

She grinned when he entered their bedroom. "Next week."

He tossed her on the bed and growled. "Next year."

And then he was moving over her, kissing her, and neither one of them spoke for a very long time.

***

As a seer, a shaman, a human with extraordinary powers, Chayton knew instinctually what he was capable of and what he was not.

But that didn't matter.

Not today.

The Pantera had gathered in the square, the square where only a few nights ago, the birth of their kind had been celebrated. Ashe had told him all about it, regaled him with stories of dancing and feasting, then begged him to help her—help the Pantera— preserve their wonderful tradition. And perhaps their very existence. They all wanted him to stop what was happening on their land, and they believed Shakpi's power was to blame. He didn't know if this was true or not. But he did know that he played a part, and that if he didn't attempt to fix what might have been broken by his hand, his daughter would suffer the stigma forever.

He wouldn't let that happen.

His eyes lifted to look at her. Isi, and beside her, a very pregnant Ashe. So beautiful, their hands clasped as they watched him. They looked so hopeful. A shock of pain went through him, weakening him, his resolve. He had failed them in the past. He wouldn't fail them now.

He slammed his eyes shut, and called upon the spirits of his ancestors. Dark thoughts and needs and wants snaked through his blood. Yes, she was here, below his feet, wanting to rise, wanting to be released. His hands balled into fists, but he forced himself to relax. Air moved over his skin, and he allowed himself, his soul, to leave his body. Sound ceased to exist, even his heartbeat, and he fell. Down, down, down, below the surface of the Wildlands, down to where she was imprisoned. Instantly, he felt rage and heat and sadness burden his mind, but he once again forced himself to relax, to be like water.

The portal was not visible to the eye, only to the soul, but Chayton knew well where to look for it. Power surging into him, granted by those who shared his blood, by those long dead, he pressed against the gaping hole, the wound, in Shakpi's prison. As expected, it pushed back.

Remaining at peace, a wave on the water of his subconscious, Chayton pressed once again. But this time, something strange happened. It was as if his soul crackled, as if lightning exploded inside his mind, and he was thrust upward, out of the ground and into the sky.

He felt the magical connection to his body break. But it was too late to do anything to repair it. He could only watch from above as tiny particles of light rose from the earth.

The crowd of Pantera gasped, some drawing back, some inching forward. Then the particles of light let out a shattering scream, surrounded Chayton's body and entered it.

Staring down at the chaos below, Chayton could only grieve his failure. That is, until he saw the eyes of his physical body open and his mouth curve into a wicked smile.

"I am free," came an otherworldly voice.

Once again, the crowd gasped. But over the din, Chayton heard the word, the name, he feared above all others, uttered by a single Pantera voice.

"It's Shakpi."

ABOUT THE AUTHORS

Alexandra Ivy is a New York Times and USA Today bestselling author of the Guardians of Eternity series, as well as the Immortal Rogues. After majoring in theatre she decided she prefers to bring her characters to life on paper rather than stage. She lives in Missouri with her family. Visit her website at alexandraivy.com.

USA Today Bestselling Author, Laura Wright has spent most of her life immersed in acting, singing and competitive ballroom dancing, when she found the world of writing and books and endless cups of coffee she knew she was home. Laura is the author of the bestselling Mark of the Vampire series. She lives in Los Angeles with her husband, two young children and three loveable dogs. Visit her website at laurawright.com